Three Kings Cartel

A Hood Love Story

A.J. Write

Three Kings Cartel

Copyright © 2016 by A.J. Write

Table of Contents

Chapter 1

Jace

My brothers and I walked out the warehouse, after just handling three of our best workers, like we didn't have a care in the world. Shit, I mean we didn't. If you went around and asked who runs the city of Baltimore, the only name you would ever hear are the Vincent Brothers. Not only did we run Baltimore and the state of Maryland, but we just about owned the whole east coast. We walked to our vehicles and stood by our passenger side doors quietly. We looked at each other in silence and did our ritual after having to handle people. We pulled out our blunts and smoked in silence while our thoughts consumed us. Once we were done, we gave each other head nods, and hopped in our cars.

My brothers, Jackson and June, and I headed towards the club. It was another ritual for us to go to one of our clubs, J5, and hang out. I'm Jace, a 28-year -old mogul in the making. I had been selling a little bit of everything since the age of 16. I didn't see myself retiring anytime soon, even, though, I had more money than I could count. Getting money had always been my family's goal. I was the oldest in my family. After me was Jackson. We have two little sisters, Janice and Janicka. Then comes June. Our motto has always been "Don't fuck with what's not yours." Our workers had to find that out the hard way by paying with their lives.

They really thought they could steal from us and not get caught. It was too bad, though, because they really had a good thing going. But we know everything that happens in our city. Nothing got past us. I was pulled from my thoughts once we all pulled up to the club. Everybody knew when they saw three or more vehicles pulling up at once then it was definitely my family hitting the scene. We all hopped out and fixed our clothes before making our way inside. And as always females and niggas was trying to get our attention, and as usua; we ignored their asses. When we stepped inside all eyes were on us.

"Ahhhhhh shit now the Vincent Brothers just stepped in the building. It's definitely time to turn up." The DJ announced once he saw us.

We gave him a head nod to acknowledge him and kept it moving to our section. We headed straight to our section in VIP. On the way there, we spoke and hugged the people we knew and ignored the ones we didn't. I guess you could say we were cocky and confident and a little bit conceited. My looks alone got the ladies' attention, but my charm was what got them hooked. When we got to our section the bouncer let us in. We dapped him up on our way in. I could clearly see that our crew was there in full swing with chicks all over the place. And I must say that they had some beautiful women in our section. We spoke and gave our signature handshake to our crew, ordered our drinks, and started smoking again.

Anyone who really knew us knew we didn't drink or smoke after anyone. We were just like that. Hell my brothers and sisters and I didn't even do that. It didn't take long for my brothers and I to start feeling our drinks, and the weed got us even higher. We were having a good time dancing and bullshitting around when the last person I expected to see was standing in my face.

"So this how we do?" Jalysa asked with her hand on her hips. Jalysa is my ex-girlfriend that I broke up with not to long ago.

"Man. Gone, Lysa. I'm not with your shit tonight. So keep it moving." I said taking the bottle of Dom to the head while looking down at her.

"But, baby. I miss you. Why do you doing me like this?" She asked in a whiny voice. I couldn't stand that shit. "Lysa, bye." I said turning my back on her.

Jalysa and I were together for seven years before I decided it was time to let her loose. I got love for the girl, but I never loved her. She was just my comfort when a nigga needed somebody by my sid. Don't get me wrong, she was a good girl. She was just not the one for me. I was damn near 30 and still didn't have any kids or a woman that was worth bearing my kids. I was ready to find me a wife and Jalysa was never wifey material for me. We didn't end on bad terms, but she was not willing to let me go since I had been her meal ticket for the past seven years. I thought she was going to be a problem but I decided to chill until she actually became one. I felt arms wrap around my waist. I turned to see that it was Jalysa. I quickly unwrapped her arms and got in her face.

"The fuck do you want, Lysa? Why are you not understanding that we are done?" I asked getting irritated already.

I didn't even listen to what she was saying as I eyed her attire. I couldn't even lie baby girl was bad. She stood a good 5'10" and had some long ass beautiful legs, but they were nice and thick like I like them. She is a beautiful brown skinned beauty with weave of course. I mean she didn't even need the shit, but she was always saying she didn't wanna deal with it, and it was easier to just have weave. Whatever the fuck that meant. Anyway she had some beautiful ass blue eyes, some shit I had never seen on a black female before. Baby girl was thick in all the right places. She has ass for days and breasts that you could suffocate in, with one of the sexiest, toned stomachs I had ever seen. Looks wise, Jalysa was the total package but outside of her looks, she wasn't shit to me and I had to let her go.

The outfit she had on was making my dick hard. I saw her lips moving, but I was still admiring her body. She had on a dress that hugged every part of what she was trying to cover up, and it wasn't much since half of her titties was spilling out and the dress barely covered her ass. But she was still looking right. *You know what fuck this.*

"Man kill all that shit you was just saying. I know what you want." I said not even caring about who saw us or how she felt.

I grabbed her and pulled her into the nearest bathroom. I locked the door, picked her up, and put her on the sink. She tried kissing me, but I leaned back on her ass. She knew better than that. I quickly released my dick, and she pulled up her dress revealing that she had no panties on. I shook my head because she knew what she was doing from the jump. I looked at her, and she had a smirk on her face.

I didn't waste any time plunging all of my 11 inches into her warm, wet pussy. Yea anytime Jalysa was in my presence her ass got wet instantly, so I never had a problem with going in. She instantly wrapped her legs around my waist and arms around my neck. She started sucking on my neck to keep from moaning but it was hard for her not to.

"Naw let that shit out, ma." I told her. She bit my neck which made me laugh.

"I don't hear you, Lysa." I said pumping harder. Shit, her pussy was feeling good. I couldn't lie her pussy was for damn sure A1.

"Ahhhhh, Jace. Shit. I'm 'bout to come." She said finally letting it out.

"Let it go then." I said slowing down. "Let me see you play with it, ma." I told her.

She leaned back and opened her legs wider and started rubbing on her clit. It didn't take nothing but a few seconds before she exploded all over my dick. I kept stroking until her orgasm subsided, and she finally caught her breath. I pulled out and walked over to the another sink and cleaned myself up.

She was still sitting there with her legs shaking and mouth open. I didn't even give her a chance to say anything, I just walked out. Her ass just wanted to cum, and I couldn't care less about cumming, so I gave her what she wanted. I headed back to our section.

"Aye, nigga. Where the fuck you been?" My brother June asked.

"Man, Jalysa showed up with that whining bullshit, so I took her ass in the bathroom and busted her down real quick." I said with a smile.

"My nigga." June said laughing and dapping me up.

I never saw Jalysa come out the bathroom nor did I care if she did. I enjoyed the rest of my night with my brothers and niggas and didn't think twice about Jalysa.

****

India

I landed at BWI feeling free, like the weight of the world was lifted off my shoulders. I was so happy to get away from California. I couldn't get away fast enough. I had been through so much in the past few years that I needed to get away for good. I was so happy that my best friend, Jalysa, was opening her home up to me, so I could get away from my ex-boyfriend, Tank. That boy was straight up crazy as hell. I wished I would've known that before I went on the first date with him, because I never would've went. That boy was a straight up stalker. I couldn't do a damn thing without him questioning me or popping up at places I was at. It was as if he didn't trust me. I gave him chance after chance until I couldn't take it anymore.

Arriving in Baltimore brought back so many good, and yet some bad, memories. I left Baltimore due to just about everybody in my family dying to the point I had no one left. I use to visit my Granmie Mai over the summers growing up so I ended up moving with her when I had no to take care of me. I was lucky to have a grandmother in California who welcomed me with open arms. I absolutely love my Granmie Mai. I hated that I was leaving her back in Cali, but she understood why I had to go. We are very close and she made me promise to call her every day, or at least to make sure I didn't go a week without calling. I definitely made that promise to her.

As soon as I got my bags and made it outside, I was hit with nice weather. It wasn't too cool or too hot. It was just right for a spring day. I was looking around until I heard my name being called. I kept looking around looking for whoever was calling my name when Jalysa finally came into view. I dropped my bags and ran over to her.

"Oh my god. I can't believe you're finally here. I swear I never thought I would see you again." She said hugging me tightly.

"Now you know I would never let that happen." I said hugging her back just as tight.

See Jalysa and I just about grew up together. Our mothers were best friends. Once my parents died and the rest of my family was gone, no one was trying to take me in, so I hadn't seen Jalysa since we were teenagers. She begged her mother to take me in, but they barely had enough room for her family. Her mother wanted to so bad, but they couldn't. I didn't understand it at the time and hated it, but now I was over it and understood it completely.

Jalysa and I talked on the phone just about every day. She kept me up on what was going on around the way and in her life. I had been trying to keep her from going into depression about her recent break up with her long time boyfriend Jace. I had never seen him before nor had I talked to him. And I don't think I care to either. Even though I knew how Jalysa was, how dare he drag her along for that long and think she wasn't going to want to fight for him back. I was ready to see what Baltimore had to offer.

"Ok, bitch, let's get going. I'm ready to finally reshow my best friend off. Momma is not going to believe it's you when she sees you." Jalysa said walking off towards her car.

I almost forgot my bags. I had to go back and get them from wherever I dropped them. When we got to her car, I stopped and my mouth dropped.

"Daaammmnnnn bitch, you riding clean as hell." I said walking around the car. She was pushing a damn Porsche Cayenne

"Oh this old thing. Jace got this for me a couple years ago. I've been trying to get him to upgrade me, but it hasn't happened." She said putting her head down and shaking it.

"Oh no you won't not while I'm here. Fuck him. He's the one who missed out on a good thing." I told her lifting her head up by her chin.

She gave me a weak smile. I could tell this break up was really getting to her. I had two options; help her get over him, or help her get him back. I just had to figure out which one was worth it.We hopped in the car and made our way to wherever she lived. It didn't take long before we pulled up to a nice ass house with a wrap around driveway.

"Well I be damn. He had you living lovely." I said. "It's aight. I've been asking for him to upgrade the house too,." she said nonchalantly.

"Why in the hell were you doing that? It's not like ya'll got kids or anything." I said looking at her like she was crazy.

"That's why I wanted to upgrade, so we could prepare for our kids." She said. I had something else to say, but I figured I'd keep my mouth shut.

We got out, and I truly admired the look of the house. Had me wishing I was living like this back at home, but Tank's ass wasn't with the domestic shit. It was cool, though, because I was so good on him. I wished him the best in life and kept it moving, but for some reason, I had a feeling that he is not willing to let me go as easy as I had let him go. When we walked inside the house, my mouth completely dropped. The outside did not prepare you for the inside. It was like walking in to two different worlds.

"Girl, close your mouth. It ain't even all that." Jay said somberly.

"Bitch, are you crazy. You are living large and you got the nerve to say it ain't even all that. You're lucky enough to have somebody get you this and let you keep it. You always felt entitled to shit." I said shaking my head.

"Yea, yea whatever. What we need to talk about is how I'm going to get my man back." She said leading me into the kitchen.

"Well can I get situated first before all you want to do is talk about this dude? I mean damn, I did just get here, and I'm tired as hell." I said yawning and stretching.

"Ugh whatever. You need to hurry up, because if another bitch takes my man then there's going to be some issues. Come on so I can show you where you'll be staying." She said rolling her eyes and leading me to my room.

Once we got there, I immediately unpacked and took a shower. I was ready to take on the city that pushed me away in so many ways. After my shower, I didn't even realize how tired I was until I got in the bed. I was out before I even closed my eyes.

Chapter 2

Jace

I woke up feeling refreshed after hanging with my brothers and crew the other night. It always takes me a couple days to recuperate. They already know how I roll, so they knew not to bother me. Being with them took my mind off the stressful shit we go through every day in the business that we're in. I sometimes wonder if I'll ever stop doing what I was doing. I was not greedy by a long shot, but I didn't want to be broke either. I wanted a family to come home to, but I wasn't in any rush to find me a lady. I do believe that when the time is right then it will happen. But until then I was going to live my life, hopefully stress free.

Jalysa had been blowing my phone up since seeing each other at the club, and I've ignored her call each time. I didn't have time for the shenanigans with her ass. She's lucky I let her ungrateful ass keep the house. All she had to do is keep up with the utilities, but we will see how long that will last since she doesn't have a job. Hopefully she saved some of the money I had given her over the years. If not, oh well. Not my problem.

I was ready to take on the day. I sat up in my bed and looked around. It was so quiet but that didn't last long, because my phone started ringing and it was only 11 am. I sighed and looked at my phone and long and behold it was Jalysa calling. I shook my head and got out my bed. I went to the shower and turned the mother fucker all the way hot. In no time my bathroom was filled with steam. Just like I liked it. I stepped in and stood under the shower head for a good five minutes just letting the water run down my body. Every time I hopped in the shower and stood under the water all the stress from the previous day, or sometimes week, released from my body.

After washing my body, I got out and wrapped the towel around my waist. I stood at my sink and looked in the mirror at myself. I admired my smooth brown skin. Standing at 6'5" with a short haircut and ripped up like an UTZ potato chip with ripples, I knew I was the shit. I stayed in shape by running daily and going to the gym four days out of the week. Sometimes more, depending on how I felt. I have brown eyes that turned hazel sometimes. My brothers, sisters, and I all look good and have niggas and bitches after us like the sun didn't shine every day on somebody new. We we're not conceited, we we're just confident as fuck.

After our mother passed from breast cancer, we were left with our father, and he was no good after her death. He became a drunk that barely took care of us. That was why I had to step up and do something to take care of my siblings. I was determined to not let us struggle. It was hard on us emotionally and mentally when our mother passed. We were all so young and it hurt, bad. From the moment we buried our mother our hearts turned ice cold. None of my siblings and I had been able to love anyone besides each other because we had no real parental guidance after our mother's death. I think that was part of the reason why I couldn't love Jalysa like, I'm sure, she wanted me to. But I know there is someone out there for me, somewhere.

I was brought out my thoughts by my ringing phone. I walked out the bathroom to see it was my brother June calling.

"What's up, JV?" I answered.

"Nigga, why do you insist on calling me the initials we all share?" He asked laughing.

"Because I can. Now what do you want?" I asked laughing myself.

"Shit. I was seeing if we was still on for the shop and a game later." He said.

"Oh shit I almost forgot but yea I'm there. I'll see ya'll niggas in a few." I told him.

"Already." He said and hung up.

June is the youngest of us all, and the clown of the family. He's also the most crazy in the family. If any of us are ever feeling low, we just call him to bring our spirits up because he always has a joke to fucking tell. I got dressed to meet my brothers. When it came to business I like to wear my suits or dress casual. But when I hang out with my family and friends, I like to keep it simple and dress down. I threw on two pair of basketball shorts, an undershirt, t-shirt, grabbed a fitted and slid on my J's that I wear when I hoop. After making sure I was looking fly and smelling good, I made my way out the door. The ride to the shop didn't take long, and I listened to the trash ass radio on the way there. Man I could rap better than half these niggas out today. Hell I could sing too, but only my family knew that. Maybe one day that one special lady might hear these nice ass vocals.

I hopped out the truck and made my way across the parking lot into the shop. On the way in, I saw a group of females standing near the shop that stopped talking once I came into their view. And with the quickness, they did what they had to do to get noticed. They started fingering their hair, fixing their clothes trying to show more skin, and putting on more lip gloss. I walked past shaking my head.

"Heyyyyyy Jace." They sang.

"Sup ladies." I said hitting them with a head nod and keeping it moving.

They try so damn hard, but I didn't get why they wouldn't let a man come to them. I never liked an easy female. I like working for it. I love the thrill of a good chase. I walked inside of the shop and it was packed and loud as hell. Everybody in the shop stopped talking and spoke to me which resulted in a head nod and handshakes to the ones I actually knew. I walked over to my barber and kissed her cheek. Yea my barber is a female, and she is the illest barber in the city.

"Hey beautiful. How you doing? You got me?" I asked after kissing Tonii on her cheek.

"Hey baby. You know I got you. You wanna wait or you want next?" She asked still cutting the person who was currently in her chair.

"You know I'm patient, baby. Where them knuckleheads at?" I asked looking around.

"You know they're in the back as usual. I'll call for you when you're up." She said.

"Ok baby." I said walking away.,

I headed to the back room where my brothers were and walked into one smokey ass room.

"Well got damn. Ya'll couldn't wait for a nigga to get here before ya'll put up?" I asked walking around giving my brother's our signature handshake.

"Shit, nigga, you know you slow as hell, but we really did just light our shits up. Have a seat, though, my nigga and light up. We got some shit to discuss." Jackson said.

"Bet. What's good?" I asked taking a seat and picking up the blunt that they had waiting foe me and lighting it.

Jackson waited for me to get comfortable before speaking. "Ok a couple things. Shit is looking good all over, but it may be time we up our shipments. We're selling pretty quick." He said while June and I nodded our heads. I was happy with that news. That meant more money in my pockets and the closer I was to stopping this shit. "Ok onto other news. Somebody is talking, but I've already got that handled. I'll let ya'll in on that later, because we know how the both of ya'll get." He said looking at us through the slits of his eyes like we we're crazy or something. June and I looked at each other and smirked.

"Fuck you, nigga. We get shit done. That's all that matters." June said putting his hand out for a dap.

"Damn right." I said agreeing.

"Any fucking ways the last thing is, it's time for our annual summer bash. You know how we do, so it's time to start planning." He said finally finishing up. June and I nodded our heads.

"Bet. I'm ready for all the naked sexy bitches." June said getting excited and rubbing his hands together.

"Uh looka here, youngin', you need to chill out this year. I'm tired of always breaking up fights, because you keep pushing up on nigga's bitches and shit." Jackson said. I sat back laughing because every year we go through the same thing with June.

"Shit it ain't my fault that once I'm in these bitches' presence they forget they have a nigga. Can't fault me for that." June said getting up shrugging his shoulders.

"BABYYYYYYY!!!" We heard being yelled.

"Welp, brothers, it's time for me to get my shit cut. I'll catch ya'll on the court in a few." I said dapping them niggas up and leaving out the room without waiting for a response. I walked over to Tonii and smacked her ass.

"Hook me up, beautiful." I said smiling.

"Jace, what the fuck I tell you about that shit?" She said through clenched teeth and holding her ass. "I'm the one with the clippers you know." She continued.

"And I'm the one that will kill you if you fuck my shit up so what's good?" I said with a smile.

"You lucky I love your punk ass. Now sit the fuck down." She said.

I sat down, and she put the cape on and got to work. Tonii is a chick we grew up with. She is the only one who I let touch my hair. We own the shop, but she runs it. She didn't think she would get business when people found out it was ran by a female, but once niggas saw my brothers and I in there then they started coming on top of the niggas that was already coming. It didn't take any time for her to hook me up. As always I paid and tipped her even though she never wants my money.

Right on cue the door opened and some kids walked in to sell some candy. Right behind them were my crazy ass little sisters. And as always there were cat calls from random ass niggas. I'm not the typical brother wanting to fuck up any nigga over my sisters. Don't get me wrong, I would kill for my fam, but they are grown; they can handle themselves. I made sure of that. Janice and Janicka ignored all the noise and walked straight over to me, kissing me on the cheek, hugging Tonii, and walking off to the back.

"Damn man. How is it having sisters that damn fine?" One nigga had the nerve to ask.

"Shit they're my sisters. I don't see what ya'll see." I said shrugging my shoulders.

Shit I knew my sisters were bad. They could pull any nigga they wanted to, but they chose to be single and do them. My brothers and I taught them well. They could play a nigga just as well as we played these females. I left out the shop to head to the store. I had to pick up some things for the house before heading to the court to play ball.

****

India

Man that sleep was so good last night. I needed that. I had`n't slept like that in a long time. After getting up and handling my hygiene, I went in search of Jay. I found her ass in the kitchen running her mouth on the phone. I stood there for a minute to see if she ever heard me walk in, but she didn't. I walked over to her and cleared my throat with my arms crossed.

"Oh shit girl. You scared the fuck out of me. Whoo. You need to make some noise the next time. Don't be sneaking up on me." She said holding her chest.

"My bad. What you got planned for the day?" I asked not really caring about scaring her.

"Nothing right now. I was just gonna chill until I find out what my boo is up to. Why what's up?" she asked. I rolled my eyes. "Don't start." She said. I threw my hands up.

"I wanted to go to the store to grab a few things. Can I use your car?" I asked her.

"Yea sure. The keys are on the hook by the door. Don't wreck my shit, Indie." She said.

"Thanks and whatever. I drive better than you." I said laughing.

"Yea ok, heffa. Let's go look at our driving records then." She said laughing too.

"Fuck you. I'll be back." I told her walking away.

With sweats, a t-shirt, and some flip flops on I walked out the house just as comfortable as I wanted to be. I was too happy that she was letting me drive her car. Not because I wanted to stunt, but because I hadn't been able to drive in a while. Jay was right, my driving was horrible but whatever. I headed to the nearest store I could fine. Jay and I had different taste in food, so I knew I needed to buy what I needed and wanted, so I wouldn't go off on her. I found the nearest Walmart and parked the car. I made my way inside and grabbed a cart. I started making my way up and down the aisles putting what I needed in the cart. I must say I was moving pretty fast. I guess I was in my zone, because the next thing I know I bumped my cart into the back of somebody making them drop whatever was in their hands..

"Oh my god. I am soooo sorry. I so wasn't paying attention. Are you ok? I can't believe I just did that." I said smacking my forehead and rambling. The person turned around and looked at me. He reached out and touched my arm which made me shut up quickly. I looked down at my arm.

"It's ok, ma. I'm still alive and I can walk just fine." He said walking around in a circle. "See." He said while walking and holding his arms up. I released a breath with my hand on my chest. "It's ok. Calm down I'm going to be ok." He said with a smile and little chuckle.

"Good. I thought we were going to have to go to the hospital or something, and I just moved here, so I couldn't pay for your visit." I said rambling again. He put his hand on my arm again. "It's ok. I'm fine." He said laughing. "What's your name, sweetheart?" He asked.

"It's India." I said a little shy. He put his hand out.

"I'm J." He said. I looked at his hand and then shook it.

"Nice to meet you. Ummm I feel bad for running into you. How can I make it up to you?" I asked.

"Sweetheart, it's ok. I'm not going to die. But you can make it up to me by accompanying me to dinner." He said. I stood there with my mouth open. I wasn't expecting that response at all.

"Uhh. Ummm. That's not what I had in mind. I was thinking more along the lines of me buying you something." I said back.

"I won't take no for answer." He said folding his arms. I looked around starting to feel uncomfortable.

"I'm sorry but I can't. Look, I'm sorry I bumped into you. Since you seem to be ok, I'll continue my shopping. Nice meeting you. Maybe I'll see you around." I said walking off quickly.

I couldn't believe he did that. I mean I look a hot ass mess. Why would anybody even want to talk to me? I was thinking about that whole interaction all the way through the rest of my shopping and back home. I must say that I was so worried about me bumping into him that I didn't get a real good look at him. When I got back to the house Jay was in the same spot I left her in, except she wasn't on the phone this time.

"Hey girl. Did you get everything you needed?" She asked.

"Yea. I did. Can we go see Momma today? I'm dying to see her and her reaction to seeing me." I said while putting everything I bought up.

"Yea, I guess. I haven't seen her in a while anyway. Is there anything you wanna do tonight?" she asked.

"Good. I can't wait. Uh naw not really. It's whatever." I said shrugging my shoulders. She instantly got excited.

"Good. We're going out, so find you something cute to wear. Or do I need to help you, because last I remember your ass couldn't dress for shit. I mean look at you now. You could've actually pulled somebody if you looked decent." She said smartly.

"Bitch please. I obviously don't since a guy did try to talk to me while I was in the store, but only because I bumped into him and asked how I could make it up." I said with a weird look on my face.

"Ooooooo really? What was his name? I might know him." She said eagerly.

"Bitch you don't know everybody. Damn." I said rolling my eyes. "Anyway he just said his name was J." I told her before she could reply. She stood there thinking as if she was going to really figure out who the hell I was talking about just by a damn letter.

"You know what? Sometimes I worry and wonder about you. How the hell are you going to figure out who I'm talking about if I just told you he only gave me a letter." I said with my hand on my hip.

"Shut up." She said back as if she just realized what she was doing. She stuck her tongue out at me which I returned the gesture. We burst out laughing. "What did he look like?" She asked.

"Ummmm to be honest. I just remember him being really tall and really cute, but I can't describe it. Hell I was worried about me hitting his ass. If I ever see him again I will let you know." I told her turning away to head to my room.

"Good. I can't wait to see him. Well, let me know when you wanna go see Momma. But we have to get back here at a good time so we can get ready. I have a feeling it's going to take some time to get you ready." She said behind me.

I walked back in the kitchen saying, "You would be surprised to see just how much I stepped up my game. Just wait and see. But let me go call Grandma Mai and then I'll be ready. Oh and after I actually put some clothes on." I told her walking away. I went up to my room and jumped on my bed pulling out my phone to call my grandmother. The phone barely rung once before I heard, "I was wondering when your short ass was going to call me. I'm glad you made it safely and found the time to give an old woman a call before I had a damn heartache. Oh and that damn blasted boy done came by here looking for you. I just might shoot him my damn self. I can't stand that punk ass little boy. Anyway, baby, how was your flight? Do you need anything? You know I miss you already, right?" You see where I get the rambling from now?

I started laughing. "Hi, Granmie. I miss you too. Yes, the flight was great actually. I felt the weight of the world being lifted off my shoulders as I walked off that plane. Oh God, well, you have my permission to shoot his ass if you want to. Hell you know I had to get away from him. I don't know why I stayed so long, Granmie." I told her shaking my head.

"Baby, we all were stupid a time or two in our life, but you just have to learn from each experience and use that lesson from here on out. I hope you really take that into consideration, baby." She told me.

" I hear you, Granmie. Well, I just wanted to call you to let you know I was fine. I know how you get. We're about to go see Momma Joyce. You know I love me some of her?" I said smiling.

"Well, alright baby. Oh I know you do. But, baby, please be careful. You know I never cared for that damn friend of yours. Just watch your back and don't be so damn naïve again.

Ok? I love you, baby. Call me when you can. And make sure you find a man to give you some, so you won't be so damn uptight. Bye." She said hanging up before I could even reply.

I love her to death and our relationship. She keeps it real with me and I with her. I wouldn't have it any other way. After thinking about what she said, I decided to go ahead and get dressed. I found something comfortable to wear and hopped in the shower again. I hated being dirty or even feeling like I was dirty. I have cases of OCD sometimes and one case is my body being clean. I don't play that. Once I was dressed, I headed out the room to find Jay, and we headed out to see Momma Joyce. I couldn't wait to see my second mother. It's been too damn long.

Chapter 3

Jace

Man shorty at the store was bad as hell. I knew she couldn't have been from here since she didn't know who I was and wasn't drooling over me like the rest of these females be doing. But damn, when I say shorty was bad in every sense of the word, that's .what I meant. I didn't normally drool over no female. And she only had some sweats and a t-shirt on, but I could see shorty's figure through all of that. She was short as shit, but I could make an exception. I couldn't believe she didn't take my offer up on going out to dinner with me. I had never been turned down in my life. Hell she acted as if her bumping into me almost killed me. That shit was funny as hell though.

Baby girl was absolutely perfect, and I only know her name. I knew I'd see her again and when I do I'm definitely not taking no for an answer. She had to be like 5'4". She had some smooth ass brown skin. And she has a lot of fucking hair, but it looked great on her. I could tell it was hers, too. I like that shit. She was thick in her own way with a handful of breasts. Shit I realized I was still standing in the same spot just thinking about her until I heard my name being called. I looked around until I saw who was calling my name.

"Jace. Hey boo. How you doing?" I heard. I frowned. Naw it wasn't Jalysa, but it was another chick I used to mess with who wais just as annoying as her.

"What's up, Tammy?" I asked dryly.

She looked as if she was coming in for a hug until I said something. "Oooo, who pissed in your coffee?" She asked stopping in mid action.

"Nobody. I got shit to do so what's up?" I asked her sounding uninterested.

"I was just coming over to speak but also to ask you a question." She said crossing her arms.

"Ok what?" I asked. "I mean. I just wanted to know what's up with me and you?" She started, but I didn't even let her ass finished. I just walked off. I didn't have time for her bullshit. I heard her calling my name, but I just kept it moving. Hell I didn't even buy anything. I just left the store and made my way to the courts. I was running late anyway. When I finally got there, I could see my brothers and crew out there warming up. I made my way to the court and as always these niggas started cracking.

"Oh finally this nigga found the time to grace us with his presence." Jackson said.

"This nigga is going to be late to his own fucking funeral. I swear if I catch you walking down the aisle to your casket, I'ma shoot your ass my damn self." June said.

"Man, fuck ya'll. I swear I got a legit ass reason for being late this time." I said seriously.

"Oh I got to hear this." Shawn, one of our homeboys, said.

"Aye, nigga, shut up. You can't talk with your five baby mommas having ass. I don't know how you have time for any damn thing." I said.

"That's cuz I got my baby mommas in check. I don't play that shit. They can try me if they want to. They know if their ass acts up they won't be getting none of that Brazilian bullshit they put in their hair, none of them wack ass nail designs they get, or them funky ass name brand clothes and purses they like to stunt around with. They know the deal. Unlike you my late ass brother. I got my hoes in check." He said.

"My nigga." June said dapping him up.

"June, you got a lot of got damn nerve when you got bitches fighting over you all day every day." I said.

"See keyword there is they are fighting. Not me. I ain't got shit to do with that. I get what I want and keep it moving. I don't fuck with none of these bitches more than once. Nobody can claim or tame my ass. And no one ever will." He said matter- of- factly.

Tommy, another nigga from our crew, stood there shaking his head. "The fuck you shaking your head for, nigga?" I asked.

"Because. I'm standing here with all you grown ass men and none of ya'll can keep a chick for nothing." He said.

"Ahhhhh here this in love, pussy whipped ass nigga go,." June said. "I'll be all that because I got something none of ya'll have, and that's somebody in my bed every night. The same person at that. There's going to come a time in ya'll life where you come across the one. Now I know ya'll situation. Hell I went through it all with ya'll, but one of these females out here is going to lock ya'll down. Mark my words." He said.

"Will somebody shut this Farrakhan ass nigga up. Don't nobody wanna hear that shit. There is no pussy out there that can lock me down. I'm not having that shit. I can't and won't deal with all the nagging and crying and emotions. Nobody has time for that shit." June said waving his hands around all dramatically.

"Ok now I'm not like them two over there. I believe there is somebody out there, and I think I found her today. Well more like she bumped into me." I told them laughing.

"What the fuck you talking about?" June asked.

"Man this little chick literally bumped into me in the store before I got here. She was rambling on and on about what happened, but she was cute as shit. I mean like fucking gorgeous, and then I asked her out because she asked how she could make it up to me, but she told me no." I said shaking my head.

"You lying. For the first time in your life you was told no. Now how the fuck does that feel?" June asked crossing his arms with a smirk on his face.

"Shit. I was shocked my damn self, but man when I tell you shorty is bad. I don't even give a fuck that she told me no. I'm going to see her again. I'm sure of that. And she said she just moved here, too. Ya'll know how I roll." I said matter of factly.

They all just stood there looking at me. "This nigga done fell in love already. I mean you always been some damn hopeless romantic and shit, so I'm not even surprised you sound like a bitch right now. I gotta see shorty to believe it. Until then I don't give a fuck what your Johnny-come-lately ass has to say. Now let's get this fucking game going. I got some pussy waiting on me." June said.

"Man your dick gon' fall off." Jackson said laughing.

"Nigga, you got some nerve. Don't even get me started on your ass. Cuz this damn bonding time will be spent on me roasting all you niggas. So what's up?" He asked smiling with his arms up. We all started laughing, because we all knew June's ass could go and wouldn't stop. I will admit, though, that the nigga was funny as fuck, but we ain't got time for all that. I came to play and whip these niggas asses real quick.

"Aye who betting. I got five bands on each game." Shawn said.

"Oh this nigga betting big money I see. You must be feeling lucky today." June said.

"Just cuz your cheap ass don't bet high don't hate. And yea you right, I do feel lucky today." Shawn said shaking his shoulders.

"Shit I'm down. That ain't nothing. Shit let's make the shit even more interesting. We'll double the amount each game we play. For you slow niggas that me ten bands the next game and twenty bands for the following. So how many games ya'll tryna play?" I asked.

"Oh ya'll niggas really fucking betting. Well ya'll know my cheap ass don't carry much money on me for this fucking reason alone. I swear ya'll niggas kill me with this shit. Who the fuck bets down payments on shit. The fuck I look like giving my hard earned money to any of ya'll?" June said shaking his head.

"Man stop bitching. We go through this shit every fucking week with you only for you to end up still playing and betting anyway. We know you'll owe whoever if you have to. Shit that's chump change to us all." Jackson said to June.

"Man, that's chump change to ya'll but that's my money. I'm not flashy and I'm not with getting robbed and shit. I don't care if we are running this fucking city. Ain't a nigga gone catch me slipping." June said getting serious.

"I feel you." Tommy said dapping June up.

I looked at this nigga and shook my head. "Your ass act like you going broke anytime soon. Nigga, you have enough money to supply a few fucking states and your ass always acting broke. Niggas know who you are re-fucking-gardless. I'm not saying I don't get what you saying, but damn, nigga, live a little." I told him walking over to him and putting my arm around him. He immediately shrugged me away causing me to laugh.

"Nigga, don't be all up on me like that. I don't know you like that." June said laughing. "

Iight niggas we been talking long enough. It's time to play." Jackson said.

"Bet." We all said in unison.

We called out to some niggas who were playing on the opposite end of the court to play against us and with that the game was on. We talked them into betting and agreed to our terms. These niggas had big money too because they were pulling money from just about every pocket they had.

We were playing for a good few hours talking shit and having fun. We were winning and everything when all of a sudden gunshots broke out. We all got down on the ground and looked around. The gunshots lasted what felt like forever, but was really only a couple of seconds. I never saw where the shots were coming from. After it was quiet for a few seconds we all hopped up making sure everybody was ok. We even made sure the niggas we was playing against was good and they were.

"Aye did anybody see where that shit came from?" Jackson asked mad as hell while getting up.

"All I saw was a black SUV. It looked like an Escalade coming from that direction." One of them niggas we were playing said.

"FUCK!" Jackson said damn near yelled.

"See what the fuck I mean. This is why I don't do the extra bullshit. Somebody will forever be coming after us and our shit." June said shaking his head.

"Jack, you know what to do man. Let's get the fuck up out of here. I'll see ya'll niggas at the club tonight." I told them dapping everybody up and dipping. I wasn't trying to be there any longer than I needed to. Obviously somebody didn't do their research or had a fucking death wish, because they just messed with the wrong ones.

****

India

We pulled up to Momma Joyce's house and like always she was outside in her garden. I got out before the car was even in park. I was just too damn happy to see her.

"Damn girl. You could've waited another minute to get out. Damn." Jay said yelling at me me. I didn't pay her ass any mind. I ran up the walkway.

"Momma Joyce." I called out as I made my way to her. She stopped abruptly and stood up slowly. She turned around even slower.

"I know that isn't who I think it is. Is that my baby Indie?" She asked.

"Yes ma'am, it is." I said innocently.

"Oh my goodness. Girl, look at you. Oh my. You're still short as hell, but you damn sure got some curves on you girl.

My, my, my you're looking good girl. How have you been? What was Cali like? Girl, come on inside so we can catch up. That child of mine will bring her trifling ass inside when she feels like it." She said grabbing me and pulling me inside not even taking a glance in Jay's direction. We walked into the living room and sat on the couch.

She hadn't changed a thing from when I was a child. "Oh my, . Momma Joyce. You haven't changed a thing." I said looking around.

"You damn right I didn't. You know how I am. I don't know why you even thought I would. Now tell me everything that has happened since I last saw you. I know your granmie misses you terribly." She said patting my leg.

"Yes, ma'am, she does. I couldn't wait to get over here. You know I missed you so much." I said reaching for a hug. "I missed you too, hunny. You know I use to wonder how you and Jalysa were still friends. You two are nothing like how your mother and I were. I don't understand that child sometimes." She said shaking her head.

"And you never will, Mother. You know that I'm your child, but you never cared about me when Indie was around, and I see that nothing has changed. I'll be upstairs whenever you're ready, Indie." Jay said at us before walking off.

I turned around to see Momma Joyce shaking her head. "I'm sorry about her." She said sadly.

"You know I always wondered what everybody was talking about when it came to her. I just say she's misunderstood. We may be different but we get along just fine." I said looking at Momma Joyce.

"Baby, there are some things you just don't know about her, and you may never know, but it's up to Jalysa to tell you. And I'll leave it at that. Now come on and tell me everything that I've missed out on. Jalysa never gave me any information about you whenever I asked, so eventually I stopped asking." She told me. I frowned my face up.

"Really? Because I would ask about you all the time, and I would tell her to tell you I said hi every time we talked." I told her.

"Baby, she never told me a thing. I honestly thought you forgot about me. Just promise me that you will be careful when you're around Jalysa. She has changed over the years, and it's definitely not in a good way. She was with that nice boy, Jace, but she didn't know what she had when she had him. She did all kinds of shit to that boy. I'm surprised they lasted as long as they did." She said with a look on her face.

Now that was some interesting information, because Jalysa made it seem like it was all him. There is always two sides to a story. I hope to meet this Jace one day to find out what really happened. I knew Jalysa could over exaggerate sometimes, but I wouldn't think she would lie about her relationship. We sat there and talked and laughed for hours. She became my mother once my mother was gone. We always got along. Hell I forgot Jalysa was even there until she came down the steps yawning and making unnecessary noise.

"Ok I guess that's my cue for us to go. It was great catching up with you, as always. Trust I will be coming by here to see you a lot so don't get brand new on me." I told Momma Joyce laughing and reaching for a hug.

"You better not be a stranger, baby. You know my door is always open for you." She told me hugging me back.

"Oh great. The door is always open to her, but yet I have to do sh......You know what, I'll see you later, Momma. Indie, you ready girl?" Jalysa said with a little attitude.

I looked between the two of them wondering where their relationship went wrong, but I'd find that out later. "Yea let's go. Bye, Momma Joyce. I'll see you later. Thanks for the talk." I told her leaving out the door.

"Don't you forget a thing I said, baby. Jalysa, I will see and talk to you later young lady." She said firmly.

"Whatever, Ma." Jalysa said. We got in the car and she pulled off immediately. It was quiet for a minute then Jalysa spoke.

"Girl, you ready to shake your ass? I need to get out. Hell I can't wait to get out." She said. I couldn't get past what the hell happened back at Momma Joyce's house.

"What the hell was that back there?" I asked her.

"Girl, nothing new. Shit has changed between Momma and I while you were gone. And pointing back towards the house. no I don't feel like talking about it right now. We can talk about it later. Now, like I said are you ready to have some fun?" She asked like what she said didn't mean a damn thing.

I sat there looking at her for a few minutes before responding. "Yea. I'm ready to let loose. It feels so good out. I love Baltimore's spring weather." I said sticking my hand out the window letting the wind blow through my hand. I was loving my hair going crazy.

"Good because we're about to have a good night. I hope I see Jace there tonight. You know they own a few clubs so they rotate between the clubs. They were at J5 the other night." She said.

"The hell? Your ass acting like you haven't been to a club in weeks or months. Hell I haven't been to one in so long I don't even remember the name of the damn club and when I went to it." I said.

"Well tonight, baby, you're going to let your hair down. Believe that. We're going to get a few drinks up in you and make sure you let loose. And don't worry, all drinks will be on me." She said.

"Cool." I said.

When we pulled up to the house and got out Jalysa said, "Pull out what you're going to wear. If you need to borrow some jewelry or shoes let me know. I got you, girl. Let's get ready for a great night." She said making her way inside and to her room. I walked to my room and sat on the bed. I went to the closet and stood there just looking at what I had. I knew I wasn't trying to wear a dress, so I was going to wear some shorts. Immediately I thought of the perfect outfit. I went and got my black, high waist shorts, pink tube top, and my multicolored pumps. The main color of the shoes matched the tube top. I grabbed my waist chain and clutch to match. Yup, I was set. I went to hop in shower and made sure I was smelling and feeling right. I got out with the towel wrapped around me and stood in front of the full length mirror. I took my time but with my eyes closed I unwrapped the towel and let it fall.

After a few minutes of gathering up enough courage I opened my eyes and looked at the one thing I hadn't looked at in months: my stomach. The stretch marks were a reminder of my baby boy that I lost at six months pregnant, not to long ago. I hated looking at my stomach, not because I felt insecure about it, but because of the fact that I couldn't be proud of the marks. I didn't have my baby with me. I would have loved to boast about what changes my body went through because of a baby but I couldn't. And my crazy ass ex- boyfriend was the reason I lost him. I was overjoyed knowing I was about to bring a new life into this world, but one faithful night ended it all. I had enough looking at it. As soon as I turned away, I felt a tear drop from my face. I didn't even know I was crying.

I went ahead and got dressed and focused on my hair and makeup. I decided to just put my hair up in a high bun and put on some slight make up with the perfect shade of lipstick to go with the outfit. As soon as I put the last item in my clutch, Jalysa came walking through the door.

"Girl, what the hell...oooooo niiiiceeee. That's hot. I'm definitely feeling that." She said nodding her head in approval.

"Thank you. And as always you're showing everything you have." I said looking at what she had on. "The dress is cute, though." I added. She was wearing a cute, blue, bandage dress that had the sides missing.

"You're such a hater." She said sticking her tongue out. I laughed and shook my head. "Can you help do something with my hair. I don't want to wear it down." She said pouting.

"So put it in a ponytail." I told her putting on my jewelry.

"But I don't have any hair out in the back." She said.

"So put something around your head. A scarf or something. I got something that can go with that, and do a bang from under the scarf. Yea that'll work." I told her.

She always came to me about her hair. I love to do hair.One day I hope to own a chain of hair salons. I know that's so typical, but I don't care. I love hair and doing it. Anyway after getting ourselves together, Jay told me to meet her downstairs. When I got downstairs she had shots ready.

"We're just taking one to get the edge off a little. It's Patron." She said handing me the shot.

"Oh shit. Ok." I said preparing myself. She held her glass up while passing me mine. I held mine in the air.

"Cheers to a good night and you coming here. May our days be good. Oh and to me getting Jace back." She said hitting my glass and downing her shot without making a face or any noise.

I stood there looking at her like what the hell kind of cheers was that. I shook my head and went ahead and downed mine. I patted my chest immediately and frowned my face up. I hadn't had any type of alcoholic drink in a long time.

"Whooooo." I damn near screamed.

"Oh god you're a light weight. We're going to have to get your ass a simple ass drink." She said walking away. After getting myself together we headed out. I surely hope tonight is a good night.

Chapter 4

Jace

After that shooting, we all went our separate ways. I went home and calmed my damn nerves. Now don't get me wrong, a nigga wasn't scared at all, but I still didn't want to leave this earth, especially this damn soon. And I damn sure didn't want to leave here without having a damn family of my own. Speaking of somebody, I hope to see shorty again soon. I went to sleep after taking a shower. When I woke up I felt so much better.

I stepped out the shower with the towel wrapped around my waist and water was dripping down my body. I stood in front of my mirror and looked at myself. My brown skin was glistening something serious. These females out here get hypnotized by my eyes. All my brothers and sisters and I look alike with certain features, but I was the only one that has brown eyes that turn hazel. To be honest we all have different color eyes. I have some amazing work of art on my arms. They all have some type of meaning. I have a tattoo of prayer hands on the left side of my chest with my mother's birthday and the day she passed. I didn't waste any time getting that tat either. I had to get it done. I needed something personal and close to me to help me remember her even more. As a matter of fact, we all have some type of tattoo in remembrance of our mother.

After looking at myself for a good while, I finally decided to get dressed to head to the club. Once I got dressed, I sat down on the bed and began to reminisce back to when we got started with our empire that we turned into the cartel. We eventually were known as the Three Kings Cartel. We supply so many states. Some of them niggas out there don't even know that they get their shit from us. We always were quiet with our shit. None of us are really that flashy but we do know how to live. For a long time, the only people who knew we were the suppliers were the niggas in our inner circle. We actually got our shit from our god father. He had been in the game for so damn long that he had been looking for somebody to take over his shit. I heard he had somebody in mind but is waiting to tell everybody.

Everybody knows who our god father iswas. His name is Big Ro. He took us under his wing years ago to show us the ropes. Ever since then things had been good. We never had to worry about a got damn thing. None of us have been to jail nor had we lost any soldiers due to unnecessary violence. Besides the niggas we did on our own them other niggas was safe. Well for now that is.

It felt good to know and see just how far we've come. I'm happy with who I am and where I am. I think my mother would have been happy with me if she was here, but she would be even more happy if I was already settled down. I knew that when I eventually found the one I was leaving the game for good. I can't risk my life when I have a family to live and provide for. Plus, our clubs generate enough money and there are other ventures I'm sure I'll choose to take on anyway.

Sitting there thinking about all of that was making me not want to go out any more, but after what happened today I knew I needed to. Looking at the time, I was running late anyway but what's new. I headed out and made my way to J5. I pulled up and hopped out giving my keys to the valet. As usual the females were trying to get my attention, and the niggas wanted to act like they knew me personally calling out to me. I dapped up the security and walked in.

"And the last Vincent Brother has arrived. It's definitely going to be a crazy night ya'll." The DJ said as soon as he saw me.

I threw my hand up to acknowledge him, and then made my way to our section. Security opened up the rope immediately. As soon as I took a step I felt hands touch me. I turned to see a smiling Jalysa.

"What the fuck do you want?" I asked in her ear harshly.

"Can I come up with you?" She asked in my ear. I shook my head no.

"Why not?" She asked frowning her face up.

"The fuck you need to come up for?" I asked.

"I mean I'm always up there with you." She said poining towards the section.

45

"We're not together anymore so why in the hell would I let you in our section? Hell I don't even know how you got in the section the last damn time." I said her with my eyebrow raised.

She looked at me as if she wanted to cry. "Why won't you just give me another chance? I promise I'll do better." She said like she was begging.

"Naw I'm good. I'm not going to repeat myself. But let me say this. There will never be a me and you again." I told her turning around to walk away. As soon as I moved, I felt her hand grab my arm.

"You'll always be mine." She said matter- of- factly and stormed off. I shook my head and kept it moving. That bitch was crazy. I finally got into our section, and I knew these niggas was about to start.

"I saw you talking to Jalysa's crazy ass. What the hell did she want?" June asked as soon as I walked up.

"The same thing every time she sees me here, wanting to come up here and talk about getting back together." I said shrugging my shoulders.

"When the fuck is that bitch going to learn?" Tommy's girl asked.

Normally we wouldn't let any females into our business, but Shameka grew up with us. Those two had been together forever. We all looked at her.

"I gotta question. Why do ya'll females act like that, though? Why the hell can't ya'll let go when it's over?" June leaned up on his knees asking wih a drink in one hand and a blunt in the other.

"I'm not about to get all deep in this shit with ya'll lame ass niggas." She said laughing. Then she looked at all of us seriously and said,"But I'ma tell you this. Everybody knows that females are just emotional creaatures. We get emotionally attached before ya'll do. Now, we'll love ya'll before ya'll have an ounce of love for us back. We're built to love. Plus, it's hard to let someone go when you've been with them for a long ass time. I mean, Jacey, you can't blame her. Ya'll were together for seven damn years. To be honest ya'll should've been married by now. I told Tommy that I wasn't going to be in no long ass relationship waiting for him to decide if he wants to be with me forever. Now granted we have been together since we were in middle school, but who gets married that young. Hell I wasn't waiting until I was damn near 30 to get married when we've been together all this time. Some females know how to put their foot down and others will go with the flow until they've had enough. I mean how long do ya'll really expect a female to sit around and wait on ya'll to get your shit together? Ok. I know we been through some shit." She said pointing between her and Tommy. That nigga started nodding his head and drinking from a bottle of Dom.

She wasn't lying when she said they had been through some shit. I understood what she was saying, but it didn't change the fact of how us males are.

"We've been through the cheating on both ends, but what do you expect when you both took each other's virginity, and want to know what it's like out there with other people. We've been through the pregnancy scares and possible outside babies. But like they say real love conquers all. If you know that is truly the person you want to be with, then you will do what you have to do to show it even if you did make a few mistakes. Those mistakes aren't on purpose at first, but then it becomes like a habit, because us women will allow things to happen and stick around thinking things will get better if we let it slide once or a few times. And you men will only do what we allow you to get away with, but ya'll can't take what you dish out, either. Once you understand and, or, find love then you will get it. I believe Jacey will find love before you two will." She said pointing at June and Jackson.

"But I don't doubt that there is someone out there for you. You can shake your heads all you want. There is somebody out there that will bring you to your knees, but I have to tell you to be careful and watch ya'll backs. I love ya'll because ya'll are my family, blood or not. You built a cartel that's not in another country and like no other. Always have each other's back no matter what and watch out for the snakes because they are around" She said stupid serious.

She then pointed to me. "Jacey, I'm glad you got rid of that bitch anyway. She was definitely a snake. They say to cut the head off and the body will fall. You need to watch her ass. She's a sneaky bitch. Please be careful out there. Ya'll better not let any damn thing happen to my baby or ya'll gone be right where he is beside him. Whether it be in the hospital or a casket. And ya'll know I'm not playing. I love ya'll." She said blowing out kisses to us all.

"We love you too, Meka. Her ass done got a nigga all emotional and shit." June said wiping pretend tears from his eyes. We just sat there and looked at him shaking oyr heads. He finally looked up and said, "What? Shit I was really crying. I don't do that sentimental shit cuz I'm fucking sensitive. That's why I can't settle down cuz if a bitch do anything to me, I'm liable to shoot her ass. Don't play with my emotions." He said seriously. And he wasn't lying. He was certified fucking crazy.

After that little moment we fucking turned the fuck up. A nigga was feeling good. I mean good. We had mad chicks in the section rocking with us and trying to be down. I could see from across the room Jalysa staring at me. But what caught my eye was the female who was standing near her. If I wasn't mistaken it looked like the girl from the market, but I couldn't really tell because it was dark in there. I tried my hardest to figure it out from where I was, but I was a little too drunk to focus.

I went to drink from my bottle when I realized it was empty. I turned around to grab another when I see June facing the corner and another pair of legs crouched down. This nigga here was getting some head in the club. I guess I couldn't talk when I got some pussy last time.

"Get that shit, June!!" I yelled holding my new bottle in the air.

He turned around and threw both arms up smiling. He had another bottle in one hand and a blunt in the other. Only this nigga would do some shit like this. I just couldn't stand these females who degraded themselves just to say they were with a nigga. I like my woman to have some respect for herself. I don't care for thots. Hell that's another reason I let Jalysa go. She thought she was slick.

Now I'm not a dancing type of nigga, but I saw the female that was standing near Jalysa out on the dance floor dancing by herself. I stood there watching her for a minute until the one song that anybody could dance to come on "Work" by Rihanna. Any thug, gangsta, or nigga, period, fucks with that damn song. I have never left our section before, but something told me to go over there and dance with shorty. I walked out the section and went straight to her not paying any attention to any of the people who were grabbing all on me trying to get my attention. I walked straight up to her while she had her back towards me, grabbed her hips, and started moving with her. And indeed it was the chick from the store. She had her hair up. I didn't know how the fuck she got all that hair in a damn ponytail, but she made that shit work for her and it looked damn good, too. Now I knew she was American, but she damn sure was moving like she was from the islands or some shit.

Her hips felt so damn good under my hands. Her ass felt good against my dick. Now I have some serious ass control over my dick, but she had my dick hard as fuck not even a whole minute into dancing. I knew she felt me, because she tensed up for a second, but then got right back into it, going even harder. Now I know she didn't see me coming, and she had been turning down dances all night long. Maybe she just had a change of heart. I didn't know, but I was glad she was letting me dance with her. The whole time we danced she never turned around to see who I was. She was just into it, and I was loving the feeling of her body against mine. It seemed like we were the only ones in the room. And never had I felt like that with any female, including Jalysa

When the song went off, I was about to say something to her, but she walked off with the quickness. I tried to reach out to her, but she was gone, switching her little ass away in them shorts she had on. I stood there and watched her until she disappeared. I finally got out of my trance, and as soon as I turned around rubbing my chin, I was looking down at Jalysa standing there with her arms crossed and mean mugging. I tried to walk around her, but she kept blocking my path.

"What, Jalysa?" I asked her.

"This what we do now? You dancing with other bitches?" she tried yelling over the music.

"Jalysa, if you don't get your dumbass out my damn face with them stupid ass questions. I'm not your man and you're not my girl. I can do what the fuck I want." I said.

"Wait. Since when did you start to dance, because your ass never danced with me." She said.

"Why the fuck does it matter now? You know what I'm done with this pointless ass conversation. Leave. Me. The. Fuck. Alone." I said trying to get around her again.

"Who the fuck was that you were dancing with, anyway?" she asked blocking my path.

"Bye, Jalysa." I said pushing her ass out the way making her stumble.

I walked back to the section with eyes all on me. "The fuck ya'll looking at?" I asked taking a seat and opening up a new bottle.

"When the fuck did your ass audition for dancing with the stars and shit?" June asked. I couldn't help but laugh at his simple ass.

"Chill nigga. That was the chick I was telling ya'll about that I met at the market. But I never got a chance to say anything to her, because she walked off before I could. Then I turned around and right into Jalysa's simple ass. What I don't understand is how Jalysa didn't see who the hell I was dancing with, because I think they came together. But I don't give a fuck. I want shorty." I said with determination in my voice.

"Well excuse the fuck out of us then, nigga. Oh hopeless ass romantic, nigga. I swear I always wonder about you," June said.

"And, nigga, I always wondered if you was really my brother. Now shut the fuck up." I said pushing him laughing.

Shameka walked over to me. "Ya'll leave him alone. He just might have found the one, and if I must say so myself I'm happy for him. Ya'll need someone to balance ya'll the hell out. Because ya'll niggas is crazy." She said smiling.

"But you dealing with the most certified nut case in the crew, though." June said.

"Aye nigga chill." Tommy said laughing.

Everybody knew Tommy's ass was crazy as hell. Him and June go tit for tat and most of the times Tommy's ass wins. The shit he has done over Meka was shit that makes you wonder why the fuck would he still deal with her ass and why is she still fucking with him. But When you have two crazy people together it must work out, I guess.

The rest of the night went by with us going back and forth with each other, but yet my mind was still on shorty. *I promise the next time I won't let her get away,* I thought to myself. Once we were ready to go, we headed out and as soon as I walked out I saw Jalysa's car drive by with ole girl in the front seat. Now I had to figure out how in the hell they knew each other, and how in the hell I was going to be able to get to her without Jalysa knowing. No, I didon't give a fuck about what Jalysa thought, but I knew how she w as, and she is a fucking handful at times. I couldan't wait to see how the hell this situation ends up.

****

India

I must say I was having a good time in the club. We were drinking and dancing when out of nowhere Jalysa walked off without saying a word to me. I wasn't going to follow her ass, but I did see her talking to some dude. Anyone looking at them could clearly see he wasn't interested in anything she was saying. In the middle of them talking some dude walked up to me just reeking of all kinds of funky smells. I scrunched my face up and put my hand up to my nose.

"Hey beautiful." He said. His breath smelled worse than how he smelled.

"Oh hell no. If you don't get your stinky ass out my face and go wash or something. Never come up to a female smelling like that. Do you not smell yourself, man? Why did they even let your stank ass in the club?" I said. "Please don't say anything else and just walk away." I told him shooing him away with my hand. He went to open his mouth. "Op no. Don't. Don't you dare say another damn word. Keep it moving." I told him pointing my finger in the direction I wanted him to go. He closed his mouth and walked off but not before mumbling a few words and mugging me.

He could've called me a bitch for all I cared as long as he kept his ass moving. Jalysa was still gone when I decided to head to the dance floor. Jumpman by Drake and Future was on and I was rapping word for word as I made my way out there. Dudes were grabbing me trying to dance with me left and right, but I kept turning them down. I just wanted to dance by myself. I was out there in my zone when I felt eyes on me. Still dancing, I looked around and saw some dude looking at me from a VIP section, but I couldn't see his face because it was dark. Slyly keeping my eyes on him, I saw when he left the section and made his way to the dance floor.

I kept dancing like I didn't see him, though. I knew it was him when I felt his body press against mine andwhen he placed his hands on my hips.. His hands on me felt natural as hell. I can't even lie. I, for some reason, couldn't stop moving nor could I turn around. The way our bodies felt against each other was something I never felt before. A feeling came over me that I never felt before and I got scared. As soon as the song was over, I walked off quick as hell. I needed a moment to get myself together. When I say an unexplainable force came over us while we were on the dance floor, that's exactly what I mean. It scared the shit out of me.

I went to the bathroom to throw some water on my face. When I looked in the mirror my face was flushed. Never had a man had this type of effect on me. After getting myself together, I walked out the bathroom to see a frustrated Jalysa.

"What's wrong with you?" I asked her.

"I'm ready to go. Are you?" She said with her arms crossed and face scrunched up.

I shrugged my shoulders and said, "Yea. That's cool." She hurriedly turned away, but made sure to grab my hand so we wouldn't lose each other walking through the crowd.

We made it outside and found the car quickly. Jay had an attitude the whole time. When we finally got settled in and pulled off, I decided to ask her what was up.

"You ok?" I asked.

"Hell no. Jace's ass was being an ass tonight. I was trying to get us in his section, but he wasn't having it, and then I caught him dancing with some bitch. She lucky she walked off as fast as she did or I woulda snatched her ass up." She said feistily.

"Girl, now you know you can't fight. I used to have to fight all your damn battles when we was young. And it's a damn good thing I know how to fight, too. You were always the bark and I was the bite." I said shaking my head. I was always fighting bitches left and right because of her mouth.

"Eh that's besides the point here. Jace's ass is being disrespectful and he knows how I am." She said angrily.

"Ok I see where this is going. You can't hold on to somebody who doesn't want you. Hell you should be thankful that he let you keep the house and car. You sure have a lot more than what a lot of these females get after breaking up." I told her looking at her sideways.

"You truly have become ungrateful. Where is the sweet girl I met years ago?" I asked.

"That bitch died the moment I got with Jace. It wasn't easy being with him. He doesn't know how to love. Hell, I barely met his brothers, and I know he has sisters, too. We never really did anything." She said hitting the wheel.

"Ok you need to calm your ass down. If you wasn't happy then why the hell would you stay so long?" I asked her. She looked at me like I was crazy.

"You know you haven't been here in a long time I don't expect you to know what the hell is going on here. So I'll let you have a pass on this one. You just don't understand. Jace and his brothers are the Three Kings Cartel. They are so well connected and have enough money to help out few villages. Who wouldn't want to be with any of them. I eventually did fall in love with him, and that doesn't make it any easier on me, because of the break up. I want another chance to prove to him that I'm actually the one. You know?" She said more softly this time.

"I don't get it. Why fight for somebody who obviously isn't worth it or wants you back? Maybe you jut need to back off and show him that you don't need or want him. I saw you talking to somebody and I'm just going to guess that, that was him." I said still looking at her. She nodded her head.

"Ok he obviously wants nothing to do with you right now. I don't know how he feels, but by the way things were looking, he wasn't and probably won't be feeling anything concerning you for a long time. So back off some. Hell maybe a whole lot in your case. Let him see what you can be and maybe he'll come back for you. I don't know but just back off. Niggas don't like that pressing, clingy shit. Hell I don't my damn self." I said shrugging hoping she got what I was saying. She sat there looking at the road then at me, repeatedly.

"You know what? You're right. I'm going to do just that. And I bet he'll be crawling back to me in no time." She said with her head held high.

I shook my head, because I just realized that this girl is crazy and would probably do some real extra shit to get him to notice her how she ants him to. This just might not turn out to well. When we pulled up the house, I hopped out, walked inside, and went straight to my room. I was ready to get in the bed, but I had to take a shower. I could still smell the guy who freaking stunk on me. Then they were smoking and all that, so I definitely needed a damn shower. I took my hair down and shook it. I love my mane. It is absolutely beautiful and easy to manage because I know how to deal with it. I hopped my ass in the shower and stood under the water letting my whole body get wet at one time. Immediately I put my hands on my stomach and thought of my baby boy. As soon as he crossed my mind the tears began to fall. I was happy the water washed them away, but nothing could wash away the pain I have felt after all this time. The only person that knows is my Granmie. I couldn't and wouldn't tell a soul about it unless they we're worthy of knowing.

After being in the shower for a good while, I finally washed up and got out. I walked out with the towel wrapped around me and got in the bed just like that. As soon as I hit the pillow I was out.

The next morning, I was awaken to a loud ruckus. I heard a bunch of screaming and going back and forth. I walked downstairs to see Jay at the door arguing with some chick and a dude standing there covering his face.

"Bitch, why are you fucking with my man? He has a girl and got damn child." The girl said.

"And? What the fuck does that have to do with me?. Ya'll ain't married so he's still fair game, if you ask me." Jay said nonchalantly looking down at her nails.

"Bitch, you done lost your mind. I followed his ass over here on more than a few occasions. If you know he has a girl, why would you still fuck with him?" The girl asked screaming.

I stood there with my mouth open like this can't be happening right now. I mean, I understood why she was coming at Jay, but then again why wasn't she more worried about what dude had done to her instead of trying to go off on Jay.

"For this reason alone. I don't have to deal with him on a personal level. It was and is just sex." Jay said wit her arms crossed.

I could tell she had a smirk on her face after saying that. I really couldn't believe my damn eyes and ears. What the hell has Jay been up to while I've been gone? I asked myself. I still couldn't believe this nigga was still standing there not stopping them. I walked up and stood beside Jay putting my arms out between the two saying,

"Whoa, whoa, whoa. Chill out." Immediately the chick stopped talking and looked me up and down.

"Who the fuck are you?" She asked pointing to me with her face all scrunched up.

"I'm the person who's going to stop this madness since somebody else can't." I said putting emphasis on the last part while mugging dude.

"Uh uh don't look at him like that." She told me with her face scrunched up.

"Shit somebody should." I said.

"Exactly." Jay said.

"Shh. Don't you say nothing else." I said pointing and looking at Jay. She shut up quick.I turned back to look at the dude and chick. Before I could say anything she just started talking.

"You need to mind your damn business. This is between us three." She said all animated pointing between her, dude and Jay.

"No it's between you and him." I said pointing at her and the dude who finally looked up. I was caught off guard by how cute he was. "And why would that be? This bitch slept with my man knowing he had a family." She said animated again. Hell every time she talked she was animated.

"Ok you're right, she's wrong for sleeping with him knowing he had a family, but also he knew he had a damn family. You should be confronting him about it since he is the one who cheated. You females kill me always wanting to confront and fight the female, and ya'll niggas kill me with letting it happen. Own up to your shit and ya'll deal with that at home. Whether she approached him or he approached her, he's still he main one in the wrong. PERIOD. So you should graciously save face and leave because there will definitely be no fighting while I'm standing here." I said serious as hell. They all looked at me like I was crazy. Then out of nowhere the dude decided to speak up.

"See I tried to tell your ass not to come over here, and let's handle this at home. I know the mistake I made. This shit is petty for us to even be here." He said shaking his head.

"Oh now you have something to say. You should've said this shit before ya'll even left the damn house. I know the only reason why you came over here was to see what she looked like. Am I right?" I asked the chick and pointing at Jay. The girl put her head down. I threw my hands up in the air. "My nigga. Is this really who you want to be with? You gotta make better decisions my dude. Now if you will, please leave." I said then I turned to Jay. "And you leave other women's men alone, so this won't happen again. Ok?" I said. She didn't respond. "Jay." I said calling her name to make her answer me.

"Ok. Ok. I won't." She said throwing her hands up in a surrendering gesture.

The girl looked at all of us and then looked back at me. "I'm sorry to you both. You're right." She said turning around.

I went to close the door and heard and saw her going off on the dude now verbally and physically. I wanted to say something, but I didn't see the point. When I closed the door, I looked at Jay and she shrugged.

"Really Jay? When did you even start bringing niggas to your house? Hell it really ain't your house. What if he wants to take the shit back, or he came over here when you had a nigga over here? What would you have done then? You gotta think, boo. You can't be acting out just because you got your heart broken. Bitches get their heart broken all the damn time. You take that shit and keep it the fuck moving." I told her wrapping my arms around her shoulder. "Now what the fuck are we going to eat?" I asked smiling trying to lighten up the mood.

"Bitch you crazy, but thank you. I can't even lie, you definitely saved my ass. I've been messing with that dude for a good ass minute now, and I know all about how his baby mother gets down. You know I can't fight for shit. She would've whooped my ass." She said seriously at first then started laughing.

"Oh I know that's why I intervened. Plus, you wasn't making the situation any better. Anyway what we gonna eat, though?" I asked again. She looked at me and then scrunched up her face.

"Bitch, you know I don't cook. Unless you cooking we're going out to eat." She said.

"Shit, I don't feel like cooking either. Ok let's go. I just need to put some clothes on." I told her walking away.

"Ok. Don't take all long and shit, either. I know how your ass gets sometimes." She said laughing.

"Whatever." I said disappearing into my room.

It didn't take me long to find something to wear. I decided to wear a romper with some J's. Yea I was cute. I put half my wild hair up in a bun on top of my head and then threw on a few pieces of jewelry. I left out the room to see if Jay was ready. Now this heffa already had clothes on, but when I found her in the kitchen her ass had on a new damn outfit.

"Really? Why did you change your clothes?" I asked her leaning on the counter.

"I think the bitch got spit on the other outfit, so I changed." She said smiling.

"You stupid for that." I responded walking away to head to the door. I could hear her ass following me, because the bitch had heels on.

"You sure you want to wear them out?" I asked turning around and pointing at her shoes.

"I wear heels out all the time. This is nothing new so get used to it." She said walking away from me and out the door.

I shook my head and followed her. We got in the car and made our way downtown to find somewhere nice to eat. It was a beautiful day, so we decided to eat outside. We were eating, talking, and enjoying ourselves when Jay all of a sudden dropped her fork, hopped up, and took off walking. I was about to call after her, but I saw that she was talking to some guy. I couldn't see who he was because his back was facing me. I just turned back around, minded my business and kept eating. After about thirty minutes of waiting on her, I went ahead and got her food put in a doggy bag and paid for our meals. I walked over towards them. As soon as I reached them the guy started walking off. Jay looked real frustrated at this point. When she saw me, she looked at me and I could see the tears welling up in her eyes.

"What's wrong, Jay? Why you crying? Who was that?" I asked turning in the direction I saw dude walk off to.

"That was Jace. I just came over to speak, and he went off on me. He found out about dude I been messing with and bringing him to the house. He called me disrespectful and some other names I'd rather not say. I don't know what to do or how to show him that I'm the one for him anymore." She said letting the tears flow. I gave her a hug then walked her to the car and we made our way home. Before getting out the car, I turned to her.

"You have to find yourself and stop going after somebody who doesn't want you. What happened to you falling back some?" I asked her curiously. She shrugged.

"I swear that's what I wanted to do, but seeing him always makes me want to talk to or reach out to him, but it's never reciprocated." She said.

"And it never will be unless you fall the fuck back some." I told her patting her leg and getting out the car. I really hoped she thinks about what I just said. I went inside and straight to

64

my room. I laid on the bed just thinking when there was knock at the door. "Yea. Come in." I said.

Jay popped her head in. "Hey I just wanted to say thank you for taking care of the food. I got it next time." She said with a smile.

"Cool. Wasn't no biggie." I replied shrugging my shoulders. She looked down then looked back up. "Thank you for that talk too. I'm going to work on it. Don't get mad, though. I'm a work in progress." She said closing the door. I laid there wondering if she really was going to change. I couldn't wonder too long, because I was out not even a minute after she closed the door.

Chapter 5

Jace

After leaving the club and seeing that girl India, I couldn't get shorty off my mind. Hell I thought about her all the way home and up until I went to sleep. I just woke up, and she was still on my mind. That girl is a straight up mystery, and I am determined to figure her the fuck out. I couldn't think about her for too long because my phone started ringing.

"Yea." I answered.

"Get to the warehouse quick, my nigga." I could hear Jackson say before he hung up.

Now at that moment I knew some shit just went down. I got dressed in my usual gear, when I know I'm about to handle some real business, and headed to the spot immediately. I could see both June and Jackson's cars when I pulled up. Right along with Tommy and Shawn's.

I hopped out and made my way inside swiftly. When I got inside I could hear a blow torch going and the smell flesh burning. I made my way inside our "Fuck Em Up" area and saw these niggas standing around somebody in a chair.

"The fuck is going on here?" I asked looking around. They all turned and looked at me, and I could see that June was the one with the blow torch.

"We caught this nigga trying to break in here and we also found out he was the one talking. The FEDs been watching us for a while." Jackson said. I walked up to the nigga in the chair and took a good look at him.

"Really nigga?" I asked recognizing him as one of our best workers.

"Was you not eating enough?" I asked him. He looked up at me.

"Man it ain't even like that." He said with his voice cracking. His face was bloody as hell. Half his skin was gone on his legs and arms. I think the only thing left in tact was his damn dick, balls, and ass.

"So what was it like then? Because if I understand correctly we all make sure our peoples eat, and well, might I add. So I'm trying to figure out why would you turn on us." I said looking him in the eyes waiting for a reply. He put his head down.

"Man they picked me up on some wack ass charges and was going to give me some dumbass time for it. You know my situation with my family. I couldn't risk leaving them." He said.

"So instead of you coming to us for help you turn on us? Is that what you're trying to tell me?" I said folding my arms. He didn't respond. So I punched him in his shit.

"My nigga, answer me." I yelled.

"Ahhhhhhh." He yelped out when I hit him. "I wasn't thinking ok. I just didn't want to leave my family. Look I'm sorry. It won't happen again. I promise." He said.

"You got damn right it won't happen again, because there's no reason for you to say another fucking thing. Make sure you tell Jerry and Spank I said what's up. Do this nigga." I said turning around.

"WAIT! NOOOOOOOO! Come on man. Please don't do this. What will my family do if I'm gone?" He yelled.

"For one you should've thought about that before you went to snitching land, and two I'll make sure they're good. The way it should've been from the jump. I'm out." I said walking away.

"Ahhhhhhhhhh." I heard from behind me. I already knew June was finishing him off without having to turn back and look.

It was silent before I even touched the door. A gunshot rang out, and I knew at that moment that nigga was done. I told these niggas to not fuck with me. Now I have to talk to my peoples and find out what the fuck was really going on. I normally got a heads up when them Alphabet boys were on our trail. I walked out and stood by my car and smoked me a blunt. I waited until them niggas was done. About twenty minutes later, I saw the clean up crew coming through. They hopped out, gave me a head nod, and kept it moving. I returned the gesture laughing. Them niggas were about their business. They never wasted no time getting shit done. Five minutes later my niggas came walking out like they didn't just kill a nigga. All of them was shaking their heads.

"What's the word, my nigga?" June asked.

"I haven't called anybody yet. I wanted to holla at ya'll first. So what the fuck is going on?" I asked. "You know we come up here randomly to check on our shit. As I pulled up I see this nigga looking through the windows and trying to get his way inside. I already knew what he was up to, so catching him like that was the icing on the cake." Jackson said.

"Iight. Well I'm glad we got that shit out the way. I'll holla at Nick and them later. I'm going shopping. Ya'll down?" I asked pushing off my car.

"Bet. I'm with it. Where we going?" June said.

"Galleria." I replied.

"We may have to make a trip out of town if shit is really crazy." I said throwing the blunt.

"Yea I know. Shit, you know I'm down for a trip out there." June said with Jackson, Tommy, and Shawn nodding their heads in agreement.

"Bet well I'm going downtown. I'll catch ya'll niggas later." I said doing our signature handshake with each of them. As soon as we were about to leave the clean up crew was walking out. They gave us a head nod and dipped.

"Them niggas don't play." Shawn said.

"Hell no they don't. I ain't never seen niggas move so damn fast in my life." June said.

We all went our separate ways. June followed behind me as we made our way downtown. We parked, hopped out, and made our way to the Galleria and shopped like us niggas do. After spending too much damn money on myself and my family, while June's cheap ass didn't buy much, we decided to walk the harbor.

We weren't walking long before the females started coming up to us trying to talk and feel all on us and shit. We talked to a few. June, of course, got most of their numbers while I kept it at casual conversation and fell back. As soon as we were about to head to our cars, Jalysa's ass popped up in my damn face.

"The fuck do you want, Jalysa?" I asked mugging her.

"I was coming just to speak. How you been?" She said.

"You can save the bullshit. I know you been having niggas in my damn house. You disrespectful as fuck. Got me wondering why the hell I kept your stupid ass around for so fucking long. Besides the sex and head your ass ain't good for nothing. Man, get the hell on with the bullshit, bitch. Leave me the fuck alone, Jalysa." I said walking off.

I couldn't believe she had the nerve to even come up to me again. I heard about niggas being in my house from one of the niggas themselves. I wanted to get mad, but then again I couldn't because that's how her ass is, just fucking trifling. I was just mad she was that damn disrespectful. If it was her house, I wouldn't give a damn but it ain't. I could've slapped her ass, but I kept my composure. I just knew June was going to start talking shit. And as I was counting down in my head this nigga started going in.

"I told your ass about that bitch. She's a snake. I keep fucking telling you. I told you to watch your back with her from the jump. You better than me cuz that bitch would be out my shit. I would've decked her shit the moment I found out she was bringing niggas in my damn house. I swear I wonder about your hopeless romantic ass. You need to find you a woman, so you can finally do all the crazy romantic shit your ass been wanting to do. Shit I need some nieces and nephews." He said.

"Why don't you have any kids the way your ass swings dick, nigga?" I asked.

"The fuck I look like having kids before you and Jackson. Plus, I like my freedom too damn much. I can't imagine me having a little one right now. I might consider the shit after you have your third one." He said laughing. I stood there shaking my head.

"Nigga, I'm going home on that note. I got some fucking calls to make. Somebody has questions to answer too." I said doing our handshake.

"Bet, my nigga." He hopped in his car and left. I hopped in mine and made my way home. When I got home I went to my office to make my calls. The first person I called was Nick.

"What's up man?" Nick said sounding out of breath.

"Nigga, is you fucking?" I asked. He started laughing.

"Nigga, no I'm in my gym. Look I've been meaning to call you, but my caseload has been bananas." He said.

"And that's why I'm calling you. I had to deal with somebody today because you haven't informed me of some shit." I said a little harshly.

"Man I know and I apologize for that. The good news is that the shit was and is minor as of now. The guy they picked up couldn't even tell them shit. They tried hard to find something on ya'll, but they couldn't. There's still somebody in the department who has a hard on for you guys though, so be careful out there. If shit starts getting too close I'll let you know, and I won't wait this time. I'll let you know if you have to get out of here, too." He said. He answered most of my questions and made me feel a little better. But I had a few more questions.

"What exactly are ya'll looking for?" I asked.

"I'm not on the case, but I can find out as much information as I can and get back with you." He told me.

"Thanks man. Make sure you do that." I said.

"You didn't do anything stupid did you?" He asked. It sounded like he stopped doing whatever he was doing.

"Now you know how we roll, Nick. Don't ask any questions you don't want the answer to." I told him.

"Just be careful out there, man. I'll let you know what's going on." He said hanging up.

I leaned back in my chair and ran my hands down my face. Damn I wish I had a woman that could relax me right about now. That shit would surely be nice. I could feel the stress coming. Never had we had any problems before, so I didn't know what was going on now. I leaned back up and made my next call.

"I've been waiting on this call." The voice said.

"So what's the word?" I asked.

"Ok that shooting that happened while ya'll was at the courts was definitely meant for ya'll. It's some niggas that came from Texas thinking they can take over. They're called The Got Em Boys. I can tell you now that they didn't do their research. As soon as we get off the phone a message will come through with the information you need." The voice said.

"Bet. Anything else?" I asked.

"Of course. Ok I'm sure you've already handled it, or at least know about it by now, but the alphabet boys are onto you. Nothing major but there's somebody in their department who has it out for you. That information will come through also when we get off the phone. They don't have much on you, but they are trying to bring you down and I mean hard. He wasn't the only one talking. There's somebody else but you'll have to figure out on your own. There is a snake amongst you so be careful." The voice said hanging up.

I leaned back in my chair again and began to think. Who in the hell in their right mind would want to turn on me and my brothers. We made sure everybody ate well. We've never had any problems with anybody. Now niggas want to come for me and mine?. They were about to find out just who the hell I am. I am the first King of the Three Kings Cartel. I almost forgot that I was waiting on that information. I looked at the phone and saw two messages. I opened them up and the first one had my mouth dropping. The FED that has it out for me was a chick I used to fuck with way before Jalysa. Hell, ir was back in high school actually. We did mess around, but nothing too serious so I don't understand why she was after me. This I had to get to the bottom of. The second message was pictures of the niggas who are a part of that weak ass crew who tried to take us out. What the fuck is a The Got Em Boys? That name alon doesn't have shit on my crew. They got the right ones, though. I couldn't wait to talk to my brothers and tell them this info. As a matter of fact I grabbed my phone and I called Jackson up first.

"What's good?" He answered.

"Get June on the phone." I said soon as he spoke.

"Bet." A couple seconds later I heard,.

"What's happening, niggas?" June said.

"We need to meet up. Where?" I said quickly.

"Oh shit. Umm. The club. We can talk up in the office. I think Janice is there now." Jackson said.

"Naw she don't need to hear this shit. But cool we can meet up there in like two hours." I said looking at my watch.

"Bet." They both said and hung up.

I got up and walked to the bar to pour myself a drink. I damn sure needed it. I had a couple drinks before I realized I had enough. I chilled, thinking, until it was time to meet up with my brothers.

****

India

When I woke up from that breakfast disaster, I called my grandmother.

"Hey baby. Didn't think I would hear from you so soon. How you doing? Did you ever go see Joyce?" She asked when she answered. As always I laughed at her.

"Hey, Granmie. Yea I did and it was very interesting I'll have to talk to you about that when I'm not in the house or I'm truly alone." I said looking towards my door just for the hell of it.

"I got ya, boo. Have you met anybody yet?" She asked. I shook my head.

"Really, Granmie. I mean I did, but I haven't seen him again. It's only been a couple days." I replied.

"Well, hunny. He'll come back around. I haven't heard from that punk ass ex of yours, which leads me to believe that he's up to no good. So you be careful." She said as my phone beeped indicating an incoming message.

"Hold on, Granmie." I told her pulling my phone away to open the message up.

It read: *You can't hide from me. I know you're not in Cali anymore. I don't know why you think you can hide from me. I'm going to find you. I told you, you will forever be mine.* "Granmie, you're not going to believe what just happened." I said a little frantic.

"What baby?" She asked very alert.

"I know it's from him. He just sent me a message. I need to get my number changed, Granmie." I told her shaking a little bit and looking around as if he could see me.

I immediately put my hand on my stomach. The memories of our relationship came forefront in my mind. I was out of it for a while until I finally heard Granmie yelling my name.

"Baby. India. Baby, come back. It's going to be ok. He's not going to find you. I promise you, baby. Just calm down." She said bringing me back.

"Granmie, I don't know what I'll do if he finds me. I can't go through that again. I lost my baby because of him." I said crying.

"India, baby, I need you to calm down for one. You're too damn strong to let some punk take you off your square. I raised you better than that. You know how to handle yourself. Don't you get all weak on me now. Do you hear me?" she said. I didn't answer right away.

"India, do you hear me?" she asked again but more stern.

"Yes. Granmie, I hear you. As soon as we get off the phone I'm changing my number. I'll text you the number." I said.

"Ok baby. You do that. Take a deep breath, baby." She said. "I love you, baby. Don't you ever forget that." She said.

"I love you too, Granmie." I said hanging up.

I called up Verizon quick and changed my number without much hassle. I texted it to Granmie and waited for confirmation from her that she got it. I went to find Jay to let her know.I knocked on the door but didn't get an anwer so I just walked in. I found her in her room balled up on the bed.

"Hey boo." I said walking up on her side of the bed. As soon as I walked up my mouth dropped. On her nightstand I saw lines of coke and a rolled up dollar bill. My hand flew to my mouth immediately.

"Jalysa!" I screamed.

She didn't move. I shook her some and she still didn't move. She just started moaning. I tried picking her up as best as I could and dragged her to the bathroom. I had tears coming down my face. This would explain why she was rough around the edges a lot more now. I put her in the tub and turned the cold water on. She immediately opened her eyes, but her body still didn't move.

"What the fuck is wrong with you, Jay?" I said to her.

She started moaning again. It took nearly an hour for me to bring her back from her high. We were lying in bed. She had her back towards me. She was so embarrassed that she really didn't want to talk, but I wasn't letting that happen.

"Jay. Talk. And I mean now. When the fuck did you start doing this and why?" I said turning to her.

"Come on, Indie. I don't wanna talk about this right now." She said like she was annoyed.

"I don't give a fuck what you want. You could've overdosed or something. I don't know how far gone you were, but what if I found you dead? Do you not know how much of a serious matter this is? You're gambling with your life here. You're so much better than that. Hell, this. Why? How did you even get started on this shit?" I asked getting mad all over again.

She huffed and puffed. "Bitch, I don't care about your attitude. As your friend you would be mad if I didn't question what the fuck was going on. Now answer my questions." I told her pointing my finger in her face.

"Fine. Fine." She said throwing her hands up. "I started when things started dwindling with Jace and I. I had a feeling he knew what I was doing, but he never said anything. For that I was grateful, because I didn't want to lose out on what I had going on. But then the habit just got worse. So I've been doing this for a while, and I can't stop." She told me. I pushed her.

"Like hell you can't and you will. Starting today you are. Where is your stash. We're getting rid of this shit right now. I'll be damned if you die on my ass or in my presence." I said getting up looking around and waiting for her to tell me where her shit was at.

"Oh you're fucking crazy. I'll finish up my stash and then stop after that, but I'm not throwing shit away. You crazy as hell for thinking that bullshit hunny. I spent too much money on that shit." She said then started mumbling.

"Don't think I won't be looking around your room for this shit. I suggest you get rid of it and not in your fucking system. I gotta get outta here. I can't deal with your ass right now. And even, though, I know I don't need to leave you alone knowing you still have this shit lying around somewhere, I can't stand to look at your ass right now." I told her walking towards the door.

"That's fucking fine. I ain't no got damn junkie. I can quit when I want." She told me folding her arms and rolling her eyes. I walked over to her and smacked the living shit out of her.

"Jalysa Rachelle Edwards, you have lost your motherfucking mind. Does your mother know about this?" I asked through gritted teeth. She shook her head no. I hit my forehead with the palm of my hand.

"I'm out of here." I said walking out.

I walked downstairs, grabbed her keys, and left out. I hopped in the car and just drove. I ended up at Druid Hill Park. I used to come here when I was younger when I wanted to think. I was sitting on a bench just thinking, not really paying attention to my surroundings when somebody ran past me so fucking fast that it knocked me back into reality. I looked up, and I was looking into the face of the guy from the market. He was leaning on his knees just staring at me trying to catch his breath. I was trying not to stare, but his bare chest was giving me life. I could see his lips moving, but I wasn't listening. He started waving his hands in my face. I finally snapped out of it.

"Huh? You say something?" I asked with what I'm sure was a dumb look.

"Yea, I've been trying to talk to you for a minute. Do you remember me?" He said still breathing hard.

"Yea I do. You're the guy from the store." I said.

"I was wondering when I would see you again, but I think you know we were around each other again after meeting at the store." He said looking at me intensely.

"Ummm yea we danced at the club. You probably thought I didn't know it was you, but trust me I did. But excuse me for asking this but what's your name again?" I asked looking at him with a face that showed I was clueless.

"It's J. I remember you saying you just moved here. Where are you from?" He asked sitting down beside me doing little stretches.

"I'm from here, but I moved to Cali when I had no more family left to take care of me. I'm back here because of a little situation I had back in Cali. It feels good to be back home." I said looking off.

"Are you from here?" I asked looking at him.

"Born and raised, baby. It's me, my two brothers, and two sisters. I don't normally tell anybody who doesn't already know me, but I run this city with my brothers if you know what I mean." He said. It didn't take me long to figure out what he was saying.

"Oh, got you. Well gotta get it how you live, right? I hope you don't plan on doing it forever. You know there's only two ways out." I said looking at him hoping he knew what he was doing.

"Oh trust me when I find the right woman and settle down then I'm retiring. I've been doing this shit long enough. I'm ready to quit now, actually, but I don't have anything or anybody to come home to, so why even put myself through it, you know? I mean I don't have a problem being alone. I just broke up with my ex not too long ago, anyway. I'm just ready for the right one, you know?" He said with hope in his eyes.

"I understand. So what happened with your ex?" I asked trying to keep the conversation going. He looked at me then shook his head.

"Man, that girl. I swear I could've choked her out some times. We were together for seven years. I wasn't trying to continue to string her along anymore knowing she wasn't the one. I know how ya'll females can get. Ya'll start getting antsy after a while when there's no marriage proposal." He said with a little laugh. I bounced my head from side to side trying figure out if that was true or not.

"I mean. I guess." I said exaggerating. "Some females are different. You have some who just likes the idea of the fairytale life and will do anything to get it. You have some who are the same but won't do anything to try to get it. You have some who are willing to wait and then you have the ones

82

who will put their foot down from the jump letting you know what it is they want." I said trying to let him know.

He looked at me even more intense than before. "Which one are you?" He asked.

"Depends on the guy. If I feel that we can make it work and make it far then I have no issues with waiting, but I'm not the wait for you for ten years kind of girl. Now if I know you're going to waste my time then it definitely won't last long. Each relationship is a lesson. You just have to learn from them." I said shrugging then looking away.

"Wow. Never have I ever met a female like you." He said.

"Well, we're all different in some way. You know?" I said looking at him.

We sat there and talked for a good while. I mean we talked until it got dark. Hell we ended up just walking around. Our conversation was simple but interesting. I liked talking to J. When I finally realized just how long we were talking, I decided it was time to go. I had to at least go home and check on Jay.

"Well, hey, it's getting a little late. As much as I would like to still talk to you, I have to get home and check on a few things. It was really nice seeing you again." I said trying to get away. I went in for a hug, but he pulled away from me grabbing my arm gently.

"Uh uh. You're not leaving me unless you say you will have dinner with me. And this time I'm definitely not taking no for an answer." He said with a little smile on his face. I turned away so he wouldn't see my smile.

"I know what you're doing so you might as well say yes." He told me smiling for real this time. I turned back around and looked at him.

With a smile on my face I said, "Fine. I'll go with you." I tried pulling my arm away but he held on a little tighter.

"Nope. I need your number. I don't know what kind of sucker you think I am, but you're not getting away from me this time and not for long either." He said matter- of- factly.

"Well excuse me. Fine; here's my number." I said calling it out to him.

After he locked it in his phone he said, "I have some business to take care of within the next couple of days, but look out for my call." He lowered his hand down to my hand, lifting it up to his mouth, and kissing it. I quickly pulled my hand away before I went pale again. Hell he already had the butterflies in my stomach going crazy, I didn't need them escaping out my damn mouth.

"Ok I'll be waiting on that call. Now don't have me waiting too long, because I'll say no when you do decide to call." I told him pointing at him.

"Yes, ma'am." He said with his hands up. We went our separate ways.

All the way home I thought about the good and simple time I had with him. I was looking forward to his call. It was time I got home to Jay to make sure her ass didn't try and overdose again.

Chapter 6

Jace

Now I like meeting up with my brothers, but not when it came to having bad news or any crazy news at all. When it was finally time to meet up with them, all I could think about was what I had to show and tell them. But I also knew that June would be ready to do whatever was needed to protect us and our family. Jackson wasn't down with the crazy shit. He's the one that tries to keep everything peaceful between everybody. I got myself together and headed towards the club.

I knew I was going to need a few more drinks in my system for this shit. When I got there as usual they were already there. I walked inside and spoke to all the workers as I made my way to the office. What many people didn't know was that our sisters runs our clubs, and they do a damn good job doing it. That was all they had to do. We kept shit in the family. Anyway as soon as I walked inside they got straight to the point. With smoke blowing out his mouth June says,

"Ok, nigga., What's going on?" Jackson took a sip of his drink and looked at me.

"Ok let me order me a drink and something to eat first, and then I'll fill you in. Wait. As a matter a fact I'll start by showing ya'll then fill ya'll in." I said pulling out the phone and pulling up the messages. I handed it to Jackson first and then walked out to order my stuff. I found the first waitress I saw, put my order in, and then headed back to the room. June was standing up while Jackson was leaning on the desk with his head in his hands.

"Tell me this is a joke, bruh." Jackson said without looking up.

"Fuck no it isn't." June said. "Bad thing is I remember who that bitch, Charmaine, is. Hell I fucked her while ya'll was messing around." June said looking at me. Jackson's and I turned our head looking at June with questionable expressions.

"Say what, bruh?" I asked.

"Yea man. If you was told she had it out for you then that's a lie. Not saying you ain't do you, bruh, but I fucked her while ya'll was messing around. When you was basically done with her, I was still fucking her. She thought we was going to be together after that. You know the shit I used to spit to the bitches back then was a lot worse than what I spit now.

"She fell for me and fell hard as fuck. I left her ass in the dust. She has it out for me. And if I know her like I really know her she's probably been trying to take us down since the day her ass started working for them. She ain't the brightest, but she's not the dumbest either." June said with his back towards us.

"Well ain't this a bitch. You got some niggas that didn't do their research on us thinking they're about to take over, and then you got a bitch who has it out for my baby brother because he didn't wife her ass." Jackson said shaking his head.

I just stood there not knowing what to do. Finding out that the reason behind all of this was over some dick and my baby's brother dick was funny to me. I wasn't mad at all. I was just glad that this wasn't over me, but then again it was because I was still connected in some way.

"Ok well that's not all. The last thing I was told was that there is somebody else talking. I wasn't told who but that they're closer to me than I think. Now that's really got me thinking, because nobody close to us would really do us like that." I said.

"Bullshit. I bet you it's that bitch Jalysa. She would do some shit like that, and you know it. That bitch is evil and a fucking snake. I kept telling you to watch yourself around that bitch. It's her I'm telling you. And if I find out it is then I'm gon' be the one to shoot her ass." June said finally turning around.

"Naw, nigga, you handle that one bitch, and let Jace handle Jalysa if it's true. Man ya'll niggas killing me. It's always a bitch involved somehow. I swear. Well, Ju, you know what you gotta do my nigga. We gon' let you handle that one on your own." Jackson said. I nodded my head in agreement.

"Bet. Oh I can't wait to get to that bitch. She gon' wish she never fucked with the wrong and right one. I got something for that ass." June said rubbing his hands together with determination written all over his face.

"Oh shit. This nigga here is about to fuck some shit up." Jackson said laughing.

As soon as he finished the door opened with the waitress bringing me my food and drink. June and Jackson ordered more drinks before she left out. We hung around for a good while before I decided I wanted to go for a run.

"Iight, my niggas. I'm out. I'm about to go run this shit off. You know a nigga gotta stay in shape for the ladies." I said smiling.

"Rico Suave ass nigga. Iight, nigga. Love." June said doing our handshake. "Love." I said back. Saying Love was our way of saying 'I love you.'

"Be safe out there, nigga." Jackson said after we did our handshake. "Bet. Ya'll let me know when ya'll wanna handle them niggas." I said turning to leave.

"Soon." Them niggas said in unison.

"Oh and we need to start planning this summer bash." I nodded my head acknoledging what he said and walked out.

I drove to the park, hopped out, and grabbed my workout bag. I pulled off my shirt leaving on my beater. I took my shoes off to pull off my jeans, went in my gym bag to bring out my running shorts and shoes. I put them on, locked up the car, and began stretching. Normally I would listen to music, but I felt the need to think and listen to nature this time. After stretching for a couple of minutes, I began jogging then leading into running. The one thing that was on my mind was that June said that he thinks Jalysa is the other person that has been talking. Now I could see how that could be, but I don't think she's stupid enough to do it.

Now that we're not together anymore I wouldn't hesitate to put a bullet between her eyes. I don't understand her reasoning if she is the other person. And if she says it was because we're not together anymore then that's truly some bullshit. Another thing that blew my mind was that this bitch Charmaine is the one who is after June and not me. Now this is but isn't funny as hell. June done got himself caught the fuck up with one of these bitches.

I couldan't wait to see him get up out of this one. My shirt started getting drenched with sweat, so I decided to take it off and hang it from my shorts. I took it off while still running, but pacing myself so I wouldn't run into anything. As I was running I saw a female sitting on a bench looking like she was in deep thought. Her hair was all over the place, but it was beautiful. It reminded me of the girl I met in the store. As I ran past her I took a look at her face since I couldn't really see it before and realized it was her. I stopped, ran back and stood in front of her trying to catch my breath and speak all at the same time, but I couldn't. Hell it took her a minute to realize I was in front of her anyway. I could see she had a lot on her mind just by her facial expression.

When she finally saw me standing there I smiled. I was still trying to catch my breath. Hell I was really trying to figure out what the fuck to say to her. Never have I ever been fucking speechless in front of a female before. I was glad that me being out of breath was a good reason to still be standing there looking stupid. The moment I opened my mouth, I knew there was no turning back. Trying to have a simple conversation turned into us having a great conversation. I learned a lot about her, and the way she thinks in which I was truly impressed. There aren't a lot of females out there that could even think straight let alone think like her. I was even more surprised that instead of being impressed by what I did and pressing up on me, she told me to be careful and think about what I was doing. I was about to ask her to marry me right then and there. I had to ask her out to eat again. I was determined not to let her get away from me a third time. When she said yes, I just knew she was going to be mine. I was going to make sure of that.

The moment I stored her number in my phone, I knew I hit the jackpot. She didn't know what she just set herself up for. I was going to set some shit up that she would never forget. I needed to handle some shit first, but I was going to give her ass something to think about. As soon as we parted ways, my phone rang and the by the ringtone I knew just who it was.

"What's up, Pops?" I answered.

"Hey there, son. I was just checking on ya'll." I heard him say. I could hear some noise in the background.

"Where you at, Pops?" I asked.

"Ahhhh. I'm finally on vacation. I finally found someone to turn the empire over to, and I took my girl on a little vacation. Feels good, son. Feels good." He said sounding happy as hell.

"Oh snap. Who did you turn it over to?" I asked curiously.

"That's a part of the resaon why I'm calling, I need you and your brothers to come to the spot in Colombia. We need to meet up and discuss a few things about some stuff I've been hearing that's been going on. You'll see then who is running things. I have some guys from Atlanta coming also. We're expanding, but I need to oversee the exchange. Something happened down there that they couldn't make our initial meeting, so we're going to just do one big meeting. I'll let you know when I need ya'll there." He said.

"Cool. Pops. Enjoy your vacation and tell Shida and Lil Ro I said what's up." I told him.

"Speaking of them crazy kids. They're graduating soon. You know they would love to see you and your brothers there." He said.

"Oh no doubt. Let me know everything and we'll be there. You know we're having our annual summer bash. Can you make it?" I asked.

"Yup. I'll be there this year. That way you can meet my lady." He said.

"Cool. I'm with it. Can't wait to meet her. I'll send you the details about it when we finalize everything." I told him.

"Ok, son. Take care." He said hanging up. As I walked to the car, I knew shit was about to get even more interesting. And I couldn't wait to see the outcome of things.

****

India

The whole way back to the house I thought about J. I couldn't believe I gave in and gave him my number and agreed to go out with him. I just hope things go well. When I finally got to the house it was quiet. I walked upstairs to check on Jay, but as I neared her room I heard voices. I got as close as I could so that I could hear what was being said.

"I told you I didn't want to do this. I shouldn't have agreed to this bullshit in the first place. When or if he finds out it's me he's going to kill me." I could hear Jay say and it sounded like she was crying.

"Forget that, nigga. You'll always have an unlimited supply if you keep this up. You know I got you. You've always had my back, so I'll always have yours." I heard a male's voice say.

"I don't think I want to do this anymore. I'm sure they know by now that something is up. They have never had any trouble before. Hell why are you even doing this?" She asked.

Then I heard a long sniff and then it got quiet. I got mad all over again. I wanted so bad to bust in on her ass, but I had to wait. I wanted to hear what else was going to be said.

"You came to me wanting to make him pay, remember? So don't act like this is all on me." The male voice said. I couldn't believe what I was hearing, and I didn't even know what the hell they were talking about. I didn't hear anything

94

else from them, so I decided to make some noise to see what she would do. I ran back downstairs quietly to act like I just came inside.

"Jay, I'm back." I yelled out.

I hurried back up the stairs and near her room to hear what she was doing, but I didn't hear anything. I went to her door and listened through the door. I still didn't hear anything. I opened the door, and what I saw made me want to throw up in my mouth. They were both naked on the bed doing lines off each other's body. And by the looks on their faces they were already high.

"What the fuck, Jay?" I yelled. They both hopped up quick.

"Shit." I could hear her mumble. As soon as the guy's face popped up, I recognized him as the same dude from earlier that was at the door with his girl. I stood there shaking my head.

"You just won't learn now, will you?" I asked. "I can't believe you. No wonder you really didn't care about that girl being here. You knew you were going to continue to mess with him and why? Because of some damn drugs, Jay? You really care about drugs that much that you're willing to throw your life away over them? If you're going to continue to do this then I'm moving out. I can't stand to see you like this. This is fucking crazy." I said throwing my hands up in the air.

All the while her and the dude were just staring at me like I wasn't even talking to them. I just walked out. I went to my room with tears running down my eyes. I really lost my friend to some damn drugs. I was dead serious about not sticking around. Through my tears I packed my shit. As soon as I packed my last item the door opened and in walked Jay with this far away look.

"What Jay?" I asked without looking at her. "Are you really leaving?" She asked with her arms crossed.

"I really am. I can't stand to see you do this to yourself. You're not the girl I once knew." I said shaking my head.

"Exactly. I'm not that girl anymore. People change, Indie." She said.

"You're right they do. But the majority of the time it's for the better not for the worse. You're doing fucking drugs for Christ's sake and not for any illnesses, but because some bum ass nigga is supplying them to you. You're throwing your life away, and I won't stand by to watch it. I'm calling me a cab." I said zipping up my bag. I put all my bags near the door. I walked in the bathroom to make sure I had everything. I looked over the room once more.

"You're not joking are you?" Jay asked. I looked at her and she wasn't even looking at me because her eyes were closed.

"I can't even take you serious right now. You're fucking nodding off while I'm talking and you don't even realize it. Get the fuck out my way Jay." I told her pushing her out my way and grabbing my things. I grabbed as much as I could at once and made my way down the steps. She stood at the top of the steps watching me.

"Indie, you don't have to leave. But I'm not the same girl anymore. I'm tired of people walking over me." She said sounding frustrated.

"Ok that's great. Then do something about it, but going to drugs doesn't help any fucking situation. It makes it worse. You're fucking up your body and for what? A quick high that you're going to forever chase. If you don't stop now you're never going to stop." I said looking at her. But I could tell I was talking to a brick wall. "Call me when you wanna hang out. I'll always be your friend, but I won't stay here or stand by when you're doing that shit. I won't." I said walking out.

I stood outside and called a cab. It didn't take long at all for them to come. I hopped in and told them to take me to the nearest hotel. With that we were off. I thought about Jalysa the whole time. She didn't know what she was doing to herself. She always thought she knew everything, and she always got herself into some shit she couldn't get herself out of. She would always come to me to get her out of the jam she got herself in. We pulled up to the hotel, I hopped out, paid, and got my stuff with the driver's help. I made my way inside and checked in. I didn't need anything fancy. I just needed a room until I found somewhere to go.

As soon as I got settled in I called Granmie. "Hey baby. Is everything ok?" She said as soon as she answered.

"No, Granmnie. You're not going to believe what kind of day I've had so far." I said.

"Oh Lawd. Let me go get me a cup so you can pour me some tea. What done happened now? That girl smoking that stuff or something?" She asked. My mouth dropped.

"How did you know?" I asked.

"Know what, baby?" She countered.

"That she was smoking something." I answered.

"Hell I didn't. I just guessed. But are you serious? Is she really?" She asked genuinely. I sighed heavily.

"Yea. I caught her earlier passed out and then walked back in the house to her doing it again. Like I don't get it" I was saying before Granmie cut me off.

"What the fuck you mean she passed out? Girl, you need to get the hell out of there. You don't need to be around that girl no more. I done told you, for years, that girl was no good, and now she done started smoking that stuff." She said.

I could tell she was probably shaking her head. I was about to respond when there was a knock on the door. I frowned my face up. I started walking towards the door but kept on talking.

"Granmie, somebody is knocking at my door. Oh wait. I did get out of there. I'm at a hotel now. I wasn't staying there not one more minute. Hell the first time I found her, I had to put her in a cold shower to wake her up. I was super mad."

I got to the door and looked through the peephole. I thought my eyes were playing tricks on me. My breath got caught in my throat. I was staring into the eyes of my ex-boyfriend Tank.

"I know you're in there, India. I heard you talking." He said.

"Baby, I know that isn't who I think that is?" Granmie asked sounding alarmed. I backed away from the door until I couldn't walk anymore.

"I told you, you will never get away from me. You're mine forever." He said sounding angry.

"Oh my god. How did he find me, Granmie? I can't believe this." I said falling on the couch.

I could hear a bang on the door which made me jump. "Open this fucking door, India. Don't make me break this fucker down." He practically yelled.

"No. No. No." I said shaking my head. Tears started to cascade down my face immediately.

"This isn't possible. He wasn't supposed to find me." I whispered.

BOOM. He kicked the door again. I was completely terrified.

"Baby, stay on the phone with me so I know you're ok. I can't believe that little punk nigga done found you. He better not get inside either. If I could move quick, I damn sure would be on my way. That little nigga got a lot of nerve." I could hear Granmie going off.

"India, baby, I just want to talk to you. I promise I'll leave soon as I'm done. You got me out here looking crazy, baby. Now come on and open the door." He said trying to sound calmer. I didn't say anything. I just held the phone even tighter. My damn fingers were starting to hurt.

"Baby, are you there?" I heard Granmie say. I made a noise so she would know I was still there. I could barely get a word out. He banged and kicked on the door for a good couple of minutes and then it got quiet.

"Is he still there, baby?" Granmie asked me.

"No. I'm about to go look outside the door." I said slowly getting off the couch.

"No!! Don't you do that. He's probably waiting for you to do that, so he can snatch your ass up. Please don't open the door, baby." I hear Granmie begging. The tone of her voice told me to sit my ass down, but the voice in my head was telling me to go to that door and make sure he was gone. "Baby, I know what you're thinking. Don't do it." I heard Granmie say.

I made my way to the door quietly. As soon as I reached the door, I quietly put my hands on the door, stood on my tippy toes, and looked out the peephole. My eyes got so big. Tank had a gun pointing at the peephole.

"India, if you don't open this fucking door, I'm going to shoot it down. Now try me." He said.

"Granmie, I have to. He's threatening to shoot the door down." I tried to whisper.

"India, I hear you talking. Open this fucking door now. If you don't open this door by the time I count to ten this door is coming the fuck down." He said.

I walked away from the door backwards. "I heard what he said. Listen put the phone down somewhere he can't find it so I can hear everything he says. If I have to I will call the police. Hurry up and text me where you are and put the phone down."Granmie was saying

"THREE." I heard him yell.

"And open the door." Granmie told me. I hurried to do what she said. By the time I got back to the door he was almost done counting. I took a deep breath and opened the door.

Chapter 7

Jace

I took my ass home, hopped in the shower, and chilled before calling up my brothers to tell them about my call with Big Ro. They were both excited to have to make the trip to Colombia. Hell, I was excited my damn self. It's always a good time when we go there. Now we we're all wondering who the hell he let take over. He always said he wouldn't take a real vacation until he found somebody to run his empire. If we weren't already running our own shit one of us probably would've taken over. I was happy to hear that Lil Ro and Rashida were about to graduate. I was definitely going to their graduation. I was very proud of them. Now I had to find gifts for them. Those were two of the simplest kids I know. I could buy them a damn basket of candy and they would be happy. I needed to call them for real to talk to them, though. I miss those knuckle heads.

It was definitely time to start planning this summer bash we always have. We always rented out a center or park somewhere. Adults and kids were welcome. We would have music, drinks, and food of course. We play all kinds of games, like basketball, dodgeball, baseball, volleyball, and more. It's always a good fucking time until some shit pops off. It was always something so I wouldn't be surprised if something happens this year. If something doesn't then I would be very surprised. I am going to invite India to the summer bash. I have to let these niggas know that she was off limits even if she wasn't my woman yet. I was going to make her mine, though. I knew exactly what I wanted to do for her for dinner.

Something was telling me to check up on my house. I hadn't been by there in a while. As a matter of fact, I hadn't been by there since I broke up with Jalysa. She thought I was stupid. I got dressed and headed towards the house I used to live in with Jalysa. I was getting a nagging feeling in my stomach the closer I got to the house. When I turned into the neighborhood, it looked like complete disarray. I was about to pull up to the house when I saw an ambulance and fire truck. I hopped out almost forgetting to put the car in park. As soon as I got on the lawn, an officer tried to stop me from going any further.

"This is my house. What the fuck is going on?" I asked.

"I'm sorry, sir. You can't go in there." The officer said.

"This is my house. My ex- girlfriend is living here. Her name is Jalysa." I said. As soon as I said her name the officer stopped trying to hold me back.

"Come with me, sir." He said pulling me along. We walked inside and I could see that the house was in shambles. Shit was all over the place.

"What the fuck happened here?" I asked looking around.

"It looks like a robbery gone wrong, sir. But we're still investigating." The officer said leading me to the master bedroom. When we got there I saw somebody sitting on the bed leaning over with their head in their hands.

"Sir. I believe this is the owner of the house. He knows the victim." The officer said to somebody in a suit and walked away.

"Victim? Does anybody want to tell me what the fuck is going on?" I asked looking around. When the person on the bed heard my voice, he looked up and if looks could kill he would've been dead.

"Trey? What the fuck are you doing here?" I asked walking closer to him. All the color drained from his face. I knew at that moment he was up to some shit he wasn't supposed to be. He just sat there staring at me.

"Trey, what the hell happened to Jalysa?" I asked him.

"Sir, do you mind answering a few questions?" I guess the lead detective, asked. He was white, fat, and was wearing one cheap ass suit. He wasn't sloppy looking; but you could tell he took his job serious. I guess I walked in on him asking Trey questions.

"Hell yea I mind, but if it will help get ya'll the fuck out my house faster then sure." I said crossing my arms but still looking at Trey.

Trey is one of my workers. I could already guess why he was ain my house, but I was also sure that there was more to the story. That nigga always had a motive for something.

"Can you answer me one question, though?" I asked.

"Sure sir." The detective answered.

"What the fuck is going on here?" I asked.

"Well, sir, we received a call about a lady passed out in her home. When the police got here, the victim was unresponsive. When the paramedics got here they determined that the victim was in a drug coma. By the looks of things here, she wasn't forced to take the drugs. We also believe that she was possibly robbed and by someone she knows, because there are no signs of forced entry." He said informing me.

I looked over at Trey, who was trying to avoid eye contact with me. "Trey. I'm not going to ask you again what the fuck happened here. Was you here when all this shit happened, or are you the reason why this shit happened? Wait where the fuck is Jalysa?" I asked looking between the two of them. Officers were walking in and out the room touching shit and doing all kinds of other shit.

"Well sir she was taken to the hospital. Would you like to know which one so you can go check on her?" The detective asked.

"Naw. Not yet. I'll get that information later. I want to know the fucking truth. What you said sounds logical, but I don't believe it not one bit." I said to the detective.

"And what reason do you have to say and believe that, sir?" he asked. "I just have them. I want my house cleaned the fuck up. Take whatever ya'll need to figure out exactly what the fuck happened here and get the fuck out. If I find anything missing in this bitch, I'll be suing ya'll asses and everybody in that fucking department will be working for me. Is that fucking understood, detective?" I said looking at him daring him to try me.

"Sir, we will do our best." The detective try to assure me.

"Can he leave with me?" I asked the detective pointing to Trey.

"Sure. We're done asking him questions." The detective said shrugging.

I turned to look at Trey and if he wished he could be anywhere else at that moment I'm sure he was wishing it. More color drained from his face. I was laughing on the inside, because I knew he was scared as hell.

"Let's go, Trey." I said walking away.

I knew his ass was behind me, because I could feel the fear bouncing off of him. When I got to the car, he was right there waiting to get inside. When we got inside the car he was about to say something.

"Save it." I said without even looking at him. I pulled out my phone to call my brothers. I called June first.

"Yea nigga. Miss me already?" He asked laughing.

"Always nigga. Meet me at the spot ASAP." I said.

"Bet." He said hanging up.

"Oh no. Why did you have to call his crazy ass?" Trey asked.

"Why the fuck are you talking to me?" I asked not even taking my eyes off the road. I called Jackson next.

"Yea bruh." He answered.

"Meet me at the spot ASAP." I said.

"Bet." He said hanging up.

The ride to the spot was quiet, just how I wanted it. I wanted that nigga scared. I couldn't wait to hear the shit he had to say. I would know when or if he was lying, that's for sure. I could see out the side of my eye that he kept looking at me. And the look he had on his face was priceless. By the time we pulled up to the spot he was shaking like a fucking leaf. I saw June and Jackson's cars when I pulled up. I didn't know how the hell they got there so fucking fast, but I was glad I didn't have to wait on them.

I got out the car and started making my way towards the door. I stopped when I realized I didn't hear the other door open and close. I looked back to see that Trey was still in the car. I walked back over to the car and stood outside the door.

"Get the fuck out." I said through gritted teeth. He shook his head no real quick.

"I'm not going to tell you again. If I have to get you myself then things are going to be a lot worse." I said. He opened the door but didn't attempt to get out. I didn't have time for the games, so I grabbed him by the arm roughly and pulled him inside of the building.

"Tight, bruh. You got us here, now what the fuck is going on?" I heard June say before he appeared. "Ok, what the fuck is going on?" He asked when he saw Trey. He looked between the both of us.

"We're about to find out. I stumbled across some shit so we all about to find out at the same damn time." I told them grabbing a chair and pushing Trey down on it.

"Talk, Trey, and if I think you're lying it's lights out for you. Now try me. Why the fuck were you at my house?" I said.

June and Jackson both grabbed chairs and sat down in them backwards. I decided to stand. I stood there with my arms crossed waiting for him to respond.

"Ok. Look, Jalysa and I been fucking around for a minute now. Towards the end of ya'll relationship she started talking a little crazy. She said she had a feeling that ya'll was about to be done, and she wanted to do something about it. "If she couldn't have you then no bitch could." Her words exactly, so she came up with the plan to talk." He said.

"Talk how and to who?" June asked sitting up further in the chair because he was leaning back some.

"Talk to them boys. Oh mind you she's been on that stuff." Trey added.

"And you haven't?" Jackson asked.

"Naw. Ya'll know me. I don't do that shit." Trey said lying straight through his teeth, because he looked away immediately.

"Well that's hard to believe when you have white residue under your nose and not to mention your money has been coming up short lately. Oh and let's not forget that your clothes are beginning to not fit your ass anymore. Nigga, you've been showing signs of being a damn junkie for a minute." Jackson said.

Now I knew Jalysa's ass was a little shady but not that damn shady. "So what the fuck was she saying and who the fuck was she actually talking to?" I asked.

"I mean. I wasn't there when she was saying the shit, but she could only say what she knew. And she got in touch with some girl she knew. Her name is uh." He started snapping. "Damn what the hell is her name? Charmaine I think it is. It's something like that."

As soon as he said her name Jackson, June, and I looked at each other. *Damn*, I thought. This shit just keeps on getting better and better. "Tell us everything, and I'll think about letting you go." I told him.

"Naw I need you to promise me. I know how ya'll get down." Trey said with begging eyes.

"Oh well if that's the case then why the fuck would you be in MY house? Not only that why the fuck was you fucking Jalysa when she was my girl?" I asked.

"I mean I asked Jalysa if it was a good idea to be in there. Bruh, I couldn't even answer that. I mean, shit, it just happened." He said shrugging his shoulders like it was no big deal. I put my hand out towards June. He immediately put the glock in my hand, I fired off in Trey's shoulders.

"Ahhhhhhhhhhh. What the fuck? Why would you do that?" He screamed.

"You better not get out that fucking chair." I said walking closer to him.

He went to grab his shoulders. "Don't even fucking move or make a sound unless I ask you a fucking question." I said pushing his arms back down. He was squirming in the chair like the bitch he was.

"Come on man. This ain't cool." He said. I shot him in his knees.

"Ahhhhhh. Man come on." He screamed again.

"Talk, Trey. This your last chance." I said backing away.

In no time I found out everything I needed to know. Now it was time to go pay Jalysa's ass visit. It was time she answered some fucking questions. Jackson called the clean up crew, and we were out of there making our way to the club.

****

India

When I opened the door, I knew I should have just closed it right back. There stood Tank looking as good as I last remembered with a damn smile on his face. Standing there with his tall light ass. He had on a fitted with a plaid shirt, some jeans and polo shoes to match. The same smile he would give me right before he gave me hell. He pushed his way inside.

"I know there better not be another nigga in here." He said looking around.

And I mean checking every-fucking-thing bathroom, closet, under the bed, kitchen, etc. I stood there shaking my head. Hell I was still standing at the damn door wondering why I opened the door. When he finally got done he came back towards me smiling again.

"Aren't you happy to see me?" He asked with his arms open for a hug.

I shook my head right before he leaned in to kiss me on my lips, but at the last minute I turned my head. I closed my eyes the second I felt his lips touch my skin. It was a touch that brought back memories I wanted to forget and made my skin crawl. In my head I was beating myself up for letting him in, but I didn't want any problems with the people in this hotel and him. The faster I got him out of here the better things will be.

"Awwww it's ok, baby. You don't have to say it, but I know you miss me. I missed you too." He said kissing me on my forehead before walking away.

I stood there wishing I had a damn gun, so I could shoot him in the back of his head. I stood there touching my stomach as the memories of our relationship came flashing across my mind. The tears started back up again, and they weren't stopping no matter how many times I tried wiping them away.

"Come sit down." He said sitting down on the couch. I opened my eyes slowly and took my time on my way to the couch.

"What do you want, Tank?" I asked finally finding my voice as I made my way over. I sat down as far away from him as I could. He scooted over to me, touching me. I flinched.

"Why are you acting like you don't know me?" He asked trying to sound innocent.

"Oh I know you alright, and I'd appreciate it if you gave me some room. How did you find me?" I asked standing up trying to make some space between us.

"Sit down, India." He said sternly.

"I'll stand, thank you." I said back.

"Sit down." He said again.

"I said I'll stand. I'm willing to hear what you have to say, and then you can leave." I told him trying to stand my ground. "I'm not that girl anymore. You won't walk all over me. I'm done with you. Why do you think I moved here? To get away from you. To leave you to the next chick. Or hell, one of them chicks you was already messing with. I'm sure they're not too happy about being away from you and you away from them. You might wanna call them to make sure they haven't shot themselves yet." I said sarcastically.

"Oh I see this little time away from me has helped you grow some balls. I'm taking you back to Cali where you belong." He said like that was the best idea ever.

I stood there shaking my head. "No. Not going to happen. No way. I'm here to stay. You can take your ass back to Cali and let one of the chicks deal with your psycho ass, because I'm done and I mean it this time. It's not going to happen ever again. There is no me and you anymore." I said looking Tank dead in his face.

He pulled his gun out thinking it was going to do something to me, but it did the opposite. It gave me the courage to stand up for myself even more.

"Tank, I'm not scared of you anymore." I said standing tall.

"Oh I see. This little vacation you took has clouded your mind. I told you, India, you will always be mine. If I can't have you then nobody will so what's it going to be?" He said picking the gun up and taking the safety off.

Without hesitation I said, "It's going to be me. Now if you would kindly leave up out of here and leave me the hell alone." I said.

Out of nowhere there was a knock on the door. He looked at me and I looked at him then at the door. "Security." We heard through the door. In my head I was thanking Jesus even though I knew this man was a straight up fucking nut.

"Look I'll leave this time, but the next time you better have your head on straight. You're coming home with me and

I'm not taking a no for an answer. So do what you have to do to get right." He said standing up and making his way over to me.

"I don't know who the fuck this new you is, but I don't like it." He continued. I smirked at him and blew him a kiss.

"Good. It isn't for you or anybody else to like. It's for me. I told you I'm done with you. There won't be a next time." I said pushing him and starting to make my way to the door but he grabbed me by the arm. I looked at him and then my arm pulling his hand off of me and continued towards the door. I could feel him hot on my heels. With a smile on my face I opened the door.

"Hi, may I help you?" I asked.

"Hi ma'am. We got a noise complaint about someone banging on the door and being loud. We just need ya'll to keep it down, or we're going to have to ask you to leave." He said nicely.

I turned around and looked at Tank. "Oh he's leaving. Thank you." I told security but was still looking at Tank.

The look on his face was priceless. I opened the door wider so that security could see him. Tank walked out looking at me the whole time, and I had a smile on my face the whole time. The moment he crossed the threshold, I closed the door so quick. I leaned my head against the door and started praying. I couldn't thank God enough for giving me the strength to deal with that man. But I knew it wasn't over not one bit. As soon as I was done praying I ran to where I put my phone down. It went to the drawer on the side of the bed that I had left slightly open and pulled out my phone. I could see that Granmie was still on the phone. I hurriedly picked it up.

"Granmie." I called out to her.

"Oh Lawd. Jesus baby. I'm so glad you're ok. Girl, I was over here praying to every god known to man. But, baby, I must say I am very proud of you. You handled yourself very well. Girl, I just knew he was going to set it off up in there. I had my Jesus piece. I pulled out my Muslim rug and every type of bible I have. Whoo Lawd Jesus I'm so glad that's over. Now I can put all this shit up. I even had every phone out to call every 911 city close to you." She said all in one breath.

I sat there laughing my ass off. Granmie can really be a trip sometimes. "Thanks for the laugh, Granmie." I told her.

"I don't know why the hell you laughing. I was dead ass serious about everything I said. I didn't put the phone down not one second. I know that nigga is crazy, and I'm sure he's only going to be crazier now that you're not the girl he remembers. All I have to say is be careful, baby. Maybe you need to go to a gun range or something and then get you your own pistol , because I can feel it in my old ass bones that it's definitely not the end of him." She said. When she said that my liine beeped.

"Hold on, Granmie. Somebody is calling me." I said clicking over.

"Hello." I said skeptically.

"Hi is this India?" A female's voice asked me.

"Uh, who's asking?" I asked curiously.

"This is Sanai Hospital. We have a Jalysa Edwards here. She gave us your contact number to." The voice said.

"Uh yea. What the hell happened to her?" I asked shocked.

First I was wondering how the hell Jalysa even got my new damn number in the first place. I never got the chance to even give it to her.

"She was brought in due to passing out from drugs. She didn't overdose but she was close enough." The female said.

"Serves her ass right." I mumbled.

"Did you say something?" she asked.

"I said, I'll be there as soon as I can." I replied while laughing on the inside.

"Ok good. She's in room 515. If you have any questions the doctor will be more than happy to answer them when you get here." She informed me.

"Thank you." I said clicking back over. "Granmie?" I called out.

"Child, that better had not been no damn nigga you had me on hold for. You can get you some later. Hell I'm still trying to make sure that psycho hasn't come back." She said rambling.

"No. No. No. Granmie, he's gone. Well for now that is. That was the damn hospital. Apparently Jalysa damn near overdosed again, but I'm trying to figure out how the hell she got my number when I haven't even given it to her yet. When I was going to I found her high as hell and never got the chance." I told her.

I heard Granmie sigh. "Baby, you're just going to have to let her be. She'll learn on her own, but I think you need to call Joyce, baby, and head up there with her for support." She said. I smacked myself on the forehead. I didn't even think about Mama Joyce.

"Ok you're right, Granmie. Let me give her a call and I'll call you later. I love you, Granmie. Thank you." I said sincerely.

"Anytime, baby, and take your time. I'm not going anywhere no time soon. And I love you too, baby. Don't you ever forget it." She said before hanging up.

I hurried up and called Mama Joyce. She's kept the same number after all the years, and I still remember it. "Hello?" Her sweet voice answered the phone.

"Hey, Mama Joyce. It's India." I said.

"Oh hey, baby. I know you're not calling about any good news, so what has my child done now?" she asked. And I could tell she was serious too.

"Well, I just got a call from the hospital saying she passed out due to drugs in her system. They told me the room number if you want to go up there." I told her.

"I knew it was only a matter of time." I heard her say.

"Excuse me, Mama Joyce. What did you just say?" I asked her confused.

"I said it was only a matter of time. Not too long ago when she came to see me she stayed for a good while, and I was happy about that. As usual when any of these kids visit me and stay, I always go behind them in their room to clean up. Well one day Jalysa stayed in her room all day. She only came out to eat and get something to drink. I didn't see her much but just knowing she was there was good enough for me. When she left she left in a hurry. I went up to her room to clean up behind her, and I found drugs. Now her behavior had been off for a while now, but I didn't think it would be because of drugs. Now I love my child, and I'll do anything for her, but I won't stand for a junkie and that's what she's headed towards being if she isn't one already. I've talked to her, but she's never listened. I'm not going up there to see her. I'll do what I do best and pray for her. Sweet Jesus." She said. I could tell she was shaking her head.

I really thought she would've gone up to the hospital, but boy was I sadly mistaken. "Mama Joyce. I just want you to know that I had no idea. But I caught her passed out earlier and then I caught her high with some guy later on. I moved out. I can't stand to see her like that. I tried talking to her myself, but I can tell she's too far gone now. She'll need some rehabilitation." I said.

"Baby, I know you didn't know. I wanted you to find out on your own, because I know how you are about her. I'm sorry she put you through this so soon of you getting here, but I'm glad you stood your ground. If you go up there to see her then just keep me posted. That's all I need are updates. If you can do that for me then I'll be ok." She said.

"I can definitely do that. I'll be going up there as soon as I can." I told her.

"Ok baby. I'll talk to you later." She said hanging up.

I put the phone down wondering where and when things went wrong in my friend's world. I knew I wanted to go up there and check on her, but I couldn't do it today. Too much had happened and I just wanted to get some sleep. I will probably go up there tomorrow. I took my clothes off, hopped in the shower, and then got in the bed. I was completely exhausted.

Chapter 8

Jace

I was so ready to go up to the hospital to talk to Jalysa's ass. What Trey told me had me wanting to kill him all over again and then go and then kill Jalysa, but I had plans for her ass. After dealing with Trey, we went to the club as usual and turned up like we did any other time. Bottles were flowing, asses were shaking, and the music was on point. We were having a good time when shots rang out. We all got down. I looked around as my crew pulled out their guns. I didn't know where the fuck the shots were coming from. but somebody in my crew did, because I could see them busting back. I kept looking around and I could see that one of the females in our section got hit. I hopped up with my desert eagles and started firing in the direction I saw Tommy shooting. My first shot hit a nigga and my second shot caught another.

It was complete fucking chaos in the club. People were running everywhere. I could see my brothers on both sides of me busting their shits too. It didn't take long for us to put them niggas down. I looked for security. and as if they read my mind, they were making their way over to the bodies to make sure none of them got away if they were still alive. We all looked around and none of us were hit. I silently thanked

God that me and my crew were good. We didn't waste any time leaving our section to see who these fuck niggas were that tried to take us out. As soon as we walked up on them, we all looked at each other confused.

"Aye. Ain't them the niggas that we played basketball against the other day?" Jackson asked.

"Yea it is. These niggas tried us." June said.

"Wait a minute. This nigga think I'm stupid." I said walking over to one of them niggas that was on the floor. I could see him still breathing. I pushed my desert into one of his bullet wounds and he started screaming.

"The fuck?" June damn near yelled.

"The nigga was trying to play dead, but I saw him still breathing. Take his ass to the spot." I said. I turned to look at security.

"Make sure all this shit gets cleaned up. We're going to have to shut down for a couple of days to get it fixed back up. You know I got ya'll. Just do what I say and everything will be straight." I told security.

As always Jackson got on the phone to call the clean up crew. Tommy and Shawn picked the nigga up and left with his ass. June and I stayed back to make sure everybody was out and ok. We looked in every section and when we got to ours we could see the body of the girl who first got hit. I pulled out my phone to call the police when we heard the sirens in the background and getting closer.

"Aye, J, give me ya'lls guns. We'll say we did the shooting. Ya'll need to get the fuck up out of here." James, one of our security officers, said coming up to us. We handed off our guns to him and he wiped them down. We made our way out through the back door and hopped in our rides.

We got to the spot in no time. When we walked inside we could hear the screams. I looked over at June who looked at me with a smile on his face. This nigga is fucking sick. I shook my head. When we got in the room, I had to cover my nose. That nigga had shitted and pissed on himself.

"Ok. What's the word?" I asked.

"Oh we found out some good information." Tommy said.

"Sorry we didn't wait on ya'll, but this nigga was talking mad greasy. We even let him try to catch a fade, but this nigga can't fight for shit." Shawn said laughing.

"Fuck you niggas. That's why you're going down whether you kill me or not. My crew is deep." He said confidently with blood coming out his mouth.

"You talking good shit for somebody who isn't going to make it out of here. Ya crew fucking sucks. Ya'll didn't even get us the first fucking time, and ya'll was in our face. So out of all the areas and people to try to take over, why us?" I asked.

"Man on the real, ya'll making mad paper. This is a good ass area so why the fuck not?" He said seriously.

"You don't have to tell us this is a good area. We been working these blocks since we were youngins, my nigga. You should've done your research now the rest of your crew is going to get bodied like the ones back at the club. I just have one question, though." I said.

"What?" He asked spitting blood.

"Was them the same niggas that shot at us at the park?" I asked Dude put his head down. We all busted out laughing.

"Ya'll weak and wack as fuck. Man light this nigga up. Tell the niggas who's already down I said what's up." I said.

And with that we all lifted our guns and emptied all of our clips into this fuck nigga. I couldn't stand a dumbass nigga. That nigga had smoke coming from every hole we put into him. With a satisfied smile, I lowered my gun. Before Jackson could even pull his phone out, we turned to hear a noise and we all raised our guns again. The clean up crew came walking up and as always gave us the head nod and got to work. We all looked at each other.

"Them niggas don't ever say shit to anybody but Jackson, but we went ahead and called them up when we were on our way here. Just yold them where and they hung the hell up." Tommy said laughing. I smirked because I could believe it.

"Aye leave them niggas alone. They do their job and keep it moving. They said what they need to talk for. As long as they get the job done, and we pay them good then there's nothing to talk about because they're good." Jackson said walking off towards them.

The rest of us left out. I did our handshake to everybody. "I'm out. I'm tired as fuck." I said hopping in my car and dipping. I didn't get far before my phone rang.

"Yea." I answered without looking.

"Damn nigga. How you know I ain't have something else to say?" June asked with a smile in his voice.

"Nigga, get off my phone with the shit. I'm tired as fuck fucking with ya'll. If you did you would've said it, or you could just say what you have to say now." I said back. Now it was late as fuck but I knew I wasn't tripping.

"Aye, nigga, did you leave already?" I asked June.

"Naw, we all still standing here. What's good?" He asked.

"I'm being tailed." I said reaching down to get my glock.

"Bet. We're right behind you. Aye, let's go." I heard June call out and then hung up.

As soon as I reached down my back window shattered and then the bullet went through the front windshield cracking it leaving a hole in it. Glass went everywhere, cutting me on my neck, face, and arms. I grabbed my glock and started busting through the back window while trying to drive. I couldn't let all my bullets go at once, but I was determined to hit me a motherfucker again tonight. For about five seconds, I took my eyes of the road and turned to see where I could shoot. I looked and took a shot at the driver. As soon as the bullet left the gun, I knew I was about to fuck something up. Even though I aimed for the driver, the truck

125

that was following me swerved and I hit the passenger who was about to hang out the window.

I watched what happened next in my rearview. I had to look back at the road since I was going damn near 70mph. . Not even a second later the truck tailing me crashed. As soon as it hit whatever it hit I could see my brothers, Tommy, and Shawn's cars behind me. I hurriedly pulled over, hopped out, and ran towards the truck. My boys did the same meeting me at the truck. We pulled the door open. The driver was still breathing but barely. The passenger was a goner. I knew I needed to get checked out. Blood was all over me, but I didn't care.

"Who the fuck sent you punk niggas?" I asked the driver devking him in his shit.

"Fuck you nigga. Ya'll some pussy ass niggas." He said trying to be tough.

"Oh I bet you a part of that weak ass crew that's been trying to take us down, huh?" June asked pulling out a knife and stabbing the nigga in his arm. Dude didn't even budge. He didn't scream or nothing.

"Damn yo, I think he's already paralyzed. That shit ain't take no time happening." Tommy said.

"See that's what the fuck happens to niggas that don't know how to stay in their fucking lane. Wanna live paralyzed or you wanna go ahead and die?" I said.

"Man fuck ya'll. Kill me." He said trying to be hard.

"Naw, let this nigga live, so he can live the rest of his life with a reminder of why he should never fuck with the Three Kings Cartel." June said.

"I hope you find a way home to tell the rest of them niggas to not fuck with us, but if they decide to we have plenty of bullets waiting on them." Jackson said.

We all walked away, but we could hear the nigga talking shit the whole time. He was going to be left there until somebody came through. The only problem was that we we're close to the middle of nowhere, so it wa's going to be a good damn while. They must've followed one of us over here and, of course, waited until we left to ride up on somebody. As I was walking something hit me.

"Aye let's go look in the truck. There may be something in there that we can find out about these niggas." I said stopping.

"Shit you right, nigga. Well, look I know you niggas are tired, especially you Jace, so I'll go back and look." June said.

"Shit I'll watch your back." Shawn said.

I nodded my head, dapped everybody up, and got the fuck on. I was ready to get home and see how deep I was cut. Hopefully it was something I could handle at home. . I made my way home, hopped in the shower, and got in my bed butt ass naked. My cuts ended up not being that bad. All I had to do was bandage them up..

****

India

That sleep that I got was absolutely amazing. It was just as good as the one I got the first night I got here. I woke up feeling like a new person. I was ready to take on the day and finally deal with Jay. I felt I at least owed it to Mama Joyce. I got myself ready and called myself a cab. I headed to the hotel's restaurant while I waited. I sat at the bar drinking when my phone rang. I looked at it not recognizing the number.

"Hello?" I answered with confusion all over my face.

"India?" I heard a male voice.

"This is she. May I ask who is calling?" I asked curiously.

"It's J. It's not too early is it?" He asked. "Oh hey. No it's fine. I'm on my way to the hospital to visit a friend." I said smiling.

I had my hair out, so I tucked it behind my hair.

"Well, I was calling to see if you would like to have dinner with me tomorrow evening?" He asked. I could tell he was holding his breath.

Without hesitation I said, "Sure. I don't see why not."

"Ok great. Where are you staying so that I can send you a car?" He asked.

"Oh no. I'm not impressed by cars and all that. If you want me to go on a date with you, you must pick me up yourself." I said meaning every word I said. He could try that cutesy stuff with someone who would be impressed by it, but I was old school thanks to Granmie.

"Well damn, tell me how you really feel and what you really want. I'm not mad at you. Well where are you staying?" He said. I didn't realize what I just told him until he asked me again where I was staying.

"Um Um. Well. Don't judge me. I was staying with a friend, but it didn't work out so I'm at a hotel." I said saying the last part slowly hoping he didn't think of me any kind of way. There was silence on the phone for a minute or so. I took the phone away from my face and looked at it. He was still there.

"Hello? J? Are you still there?" I asked.

"Yea I'm here. I was waiting on you to tell me where you are staying. Baby, I don't care about all of that. We can figure that out later. But right now I'm just worried about doing what you asked of me." He said smoothly. I had to clear my throat, because I almost choked on my drink. Hell I almost forgot about my cab. I hurriedly paid for my drink and went outside just in time to see the cab pulling up. I hopped in and finally found my face after it dropped.

"India, Ma? You still there?" He asked.

"Um yea I'm still here. I'm at the Sheraton downtown." I finally answered.

"Ok good. I'll be there at eight pm." He said.

"Uh ok. I guess call me when you're on your way." I said.

"Cool. I can do that. You have a great day, beautiful. If anything changes I'll call and let you know." He said ever so smoothly.

"Ok." Was all I could say.

I hung up the phone and sat it in my lap. I wasn't too sure if I was ready for what he was wulling to giving. I could be pretty damn demanding but be a quiet chick, and he seemed very demanding his damn self. Before I knew it we were pulling up to the hospital. I got out but not before paying the driver. I smiled and made my way inside. I was glad the person who called me told me the room number, because the receptionist didn't look too pleasant at all. I made my way up to Jay's room. When I got there I could hear her talking. I took it as her being on the phone.

"I don't know where he is. He hasn't been answering his phone. I hope nothing happened to him." She said. I knocked on the door before entering.

"Hey girl." I said making my presence known.

She looked up at me shocked and quickly put her phone down. "Hey girl." She said so fake with a phony ass smile.

"Ok. I know fakeness when I see it, so why would you have them call me if you didn't want me to actually come?" I asked folding my arms.

"Uh I don't know. I was just scared and knew that you would actually be the only one to come." She said looking sad. If I didn't know her I would have actually felt bad for her.

"Bitch, don't get cute with me. I know you. What the fuck happened this time? I mean, I was already told why you're here, but I just want to hear it from you." I said crossing my arms.

"Don't ask questions you don't want the answer to." She said smartly rolling her neck.

"Are you serious right now. You're really out of control. I'm really only here because of your mother. Hell she didn't even want to come. And how the fuck did you get my number? I just changed it and didn't even get a chance to give it to you." I said.

She looked away. That let me know that she was up to something. "Jalysa Rachelle Edwards. Talk and talk now." I said damn near yelling.

"Keep your voice down." She said back.

"Fuck you and your demands. Now tell me what the fuck is going on." I said.

"I know Tank. Ok? Tank was the one who gave it to me." She said nonchalantly.

"What the fuck? How the fuck do you know Tank? And hell, how did he have my new number? " I asked.

"Ugh. Must you know every damn thing?" She asked like she was getting frustrated. I walked over to her and slapped the fuck out of her.

"How fucking dare you, Jalysa. I have been your friend when nobody wanted to. I have been your friend when people have told me for years not to. Hell even your own mother wonders why we're friends, and how we're still friends. I thought I knew you, but I don't know you at all. I have done for you way more than you have done for me. The only thing I never let you do is walk over me. I may be quiet, but I ain't no bitch. You have a lot of fucking nerve trying to turn on me, and you can't even fight your own battles. A real bitch would've squared the fuck up just now from getting slapped. But you a scary bitch. You know what? I'm completely done with you. Don't call or contact me again. And if I find out you've contacted or talked to Tank again, I'll whip your ass like I should've a long damn time ago." I said turning to leave out.

"Wait. What do you mean you're done with me? Girl, I made you. Nobody wanted to be your damn friend. I was the cool one. And I'm going to get my man back with or without your help. And don't worry about how I know Tank. Just know that you can't hide from him." She said with a smirk.

I stopped when she started talking. By the time she was finished I was back in her face. "Jalysa, you have a lot of fucking balls talking to me like that. You know how I am and how bad my temper can get, and you're pushing my fucking buttons. Keep trying me and you're going to be in here for another reason. You know I couldn't care fucking less about anybody being my fucking friend. I didn't ask for your fucking friendship, I wouldn't and won't ask for anybody else's. You got me completely fucked up. You deserve a good ass whooping. I hope Jace see's you for who you really are, and is completely done with your ass. And whatever the fuck you're up to, I hope you get caught the fuck up. And if you know what's good for you, which you don't, you would leave Tank's ass where you found him. He's no good, but you're no good too, so I guess ya'll would work well together. Try me, Jalysa, and you'll see a side of me you've never seen before." I said directly in her face.

I pushed her head back with my finger and walked away. I left out with such an attitude. I could hear her trying to talk shit, but I kept it moving I was completely through with her ass. I walked out the hospital and decided to give Mama Joyce a call to update her on what just happened.

"Hey, baby. Is everything ok?" She asked. "Yes ma'am, everything is ok. Well no it isn't. I came up to the hospital to see Jay, and it didn't turn out well. Let's just say our friendship is now nonexistent." I said sighing.

"Baby, I'm not surprised. It was only a matter of time. I'm sure her mouth got her in trouble." She said sounding disappointed.

"Mama Joyce, I don't understand where she's gone wrong. I just don't get it. I mean she completely turned on me as if I did something to her. You know me and you know me well nough to know that I don't do anything to or mess with anybody." I said beginning to get frustrated myself. I had my hand on my forehead walking around when I felt a tap on my shoulder. "Mama Joyce, can I call you back?" I asked looking at the person in the eyes.

"Sure, baby. Take your time." She said. I took the phone away from my face and put it in my bag. I looked back up and my words were caught up in my throat.

Chapter 9

Jace

Man I hadn't slept that damn good in a long time. As soon as I woke up my phone was ringing. Something told me to answer it. I looked at my phone and saw it was Lil Ro. I smiled.

"Lil nigga. What's good with you, boy?" I asked. "What's happening? Long time no talk, man. Are you coming to me and Big Baby's graduation? You know we would love to see you there." He said.

"Lil nigga, you know I'm in there. I talked to Pops the other day and he mentioned it. You coming through for the Summer Bash? I know you got a couple hunnies to be seen on your arm." I said laughing. I knew how that little boy got down. He got it from his father

"Man I'm only bringing one and it's wifey." He said.

"The fuck you just say, nigga? I know you haven't settled down. Nigga, you got your whole life ahead of you." I said.

"I know man but this girl here has done the ultimate thing to be down with me. I have so much respect for her. I fell for her little ass too. I have no choice but to see where it goes, but I already know this is it for me. I can't wait for you to meet her. Oh and you know Big Baby and Blake finally got together, right?" He said.

"Man, hold up. I haven't gotten past all the shit you just said before mentioning baby girl. Nigga, you mad younger than me talking like a grown ass man. I really gotta meet this girl now. And it's about time those two got it right. Hell man ya'll growing up too damn fast for me." I said.

I was happy for my god brother and sister but damn. How the hell did they have somebody and I didn't? Plus, they were talking about who they had was the one.

"Well man, shit happens, I guess. I'm happy to be going to Colombia, tho. I'm taking my girl with me so whichever comes first I can't wait to see you, Jackson, and June, especially June's crazy ass. He stay having me rolling." He said laughing. I smiled.

"That's because that nigga is stupid for real. I always wonder about him." I said laughing my damn self. Ro was still laughing.

"Man it was good talking to you. I'm sure you have some business to take care of. I just wanted to invite you to our graduation. I'll tell Big Baby about the Summer Bash. We'll be there. Oh and I definitely can't wait until you find out who's taking over for Pops, and for you to see his girl. Shit has been crazy around these parts, but it's been quiet for now. You know how that goes." He said.

"Yea man I know how it goes. Well look I'm in there. Ya'll just keep me posted on everything. Love, bruh." I told him. Yea we even got Lil Ro saying it too.

"One Love." He replied and hung up.

I was just amazed at how much those kids had grown up on me, but I was definitely proud of them. Now he really had me wondering who Pops had taken over. This trip to Colombia should be fun. After sitting on the bed for a few more minutes thinking, I decided to call India to ask her to go to dinner with me tomorrow. I already had everything set up for us. We just had to show up. I planned on sending a car to pick her up, but she shot that down real quick. I had to think of something quick to say, because she was a little feisty but I liked it. When I finally responded she wasn't ready for what I had to say. Left her ass speechless just like I wanted to. After getting her straight, I finally got up to get dressed to go see Jalysa. I needed some fucking answers and quick. That chick has been a thorn in my side for a while now. I got up, hopped in the shower, and got dressed. I made sure I had what I needed and headed out. I made my way to the hospital. As I pulled into the garage, I saw a familiar face and body.

I smiled as I parked my car. Even though she told me she was visiting a friend in the hospital, I didn't think we would run into each other at the same hospital. As I got closer, I could see that she was on the phone talking. She didn't look too happy either. I got out the car and headed towards her. As

I got closer she turned around and looked at me. The look on her face was priceless. She hung up the phone and smiled.

"Hey. What are you doing here?" She asked looking up at me.

I reached in for a hug that she returned it. She felt so good in my arms. Her hair was wild again, so I took a whiff of it, and it smelled like mangos and strawberries. I had never smelled anything like it. When we released each other we just stared at each other for a minute.

"I'm here to visit my ex- girlfriend." I said truthfully.

"Oh." She replied looking away.

"No, it's not like that. To be honest I couldn't care fucking less about her, but she's into some shit that involves me and I have a few questions for her. That's all. I won't even be in here long. I can't stand her ass no way." I said explaining myself for some reason..

"Oh ok. Well I don't want to hold you up." She said as if I was aboutto let her out my sight that quick.

"You're not. I'm in no hurry to get up there." I said hoping to keep her around.

"Well I have a few things I need to do before heading back to the hotel." She said.

"Oh alright then. I'll give you a call later." I said feeling a little disappointed that she wanted to leave so soon.

I reaching in for hug. She hugged me back and walked away quickly. I hoped she didn't think anything was going on between me and Jalysa. I made my way inside and stopped at the reception desk.

"Hi cutie. How can I help you, help me, help you?" The receptionist asked as soon as I got to the desk. I shook my head.

"Yes, can you tell me where Jalysa Edwards' room is please." I said. The receptionist rolled her eyes and looked up the room quietly. "She's in room 515." She said smartly, rolling her eyes again.

"Thank you." I said.

"Mhmm." She said not even looking at me. I walked away and made my way to Jalysa's room. When I got there I knocked on the door.

"Bitch, if you came back to talk more shit you can fucking save it and leave right back out." She called out when I walked in.

"Well it's a good thing I'm not that bitch, huh?" I asked appearing in front of her.

Jalysa looked up so quick. She smiled so wide. "Oh my god. You came to see me." She said getting up and coming towards me.

"Sit down, Jalysa. Trust me if you wasn't sticking your nose in shit you wasn't supposed to I wouldn't be here." I said seriously. The smile she had on her face dropped quick.

"Wha-wha-what you talking about, baby?" She said trying to sound innocent.

"Don't try to insult my intelligence, Jalysa. How do you know Trey, and why the fuck was he in my house?" I asked through gritted teeth. She turned sitting all the way on the bed, and I saw that her cheek was red as hell. "Damn, what the fuck happened to your face?" I asked

. "A bitch who use to be my friend was here and slapped me." She said.

"So you just let a chick slap your ass? I mean I know you can't fight, but damn, you just let somebody slap you?" I asked amused.

"Fuck you, Jace. Ok. Fuck you." She said folding her arms.

"You did that already; so no thank you. Now answer my fucking question." I said walking closer. She looked up at me, and the look on her face let me know that whatever she was into she was in deep.

"I met him when we was still together. I promise I wasn't fucking him while we were together, though." She said pleadingly.

"Save it, Jalysa. I know you're lying. And I couldn't care less if you were. You're not my problem anymore." I told her for the millionth time.

She looked at me sadly. "Why do you keep doing me like this. You know we work well together. Why won't you just give me another chance?" She asked getting on her knees begging.

"Jalysa, I'm not here for all that bullshit you talking. I want the answers to my questions. And if I don't get the truth, I'll have your ass removed from my house. You know you have nowhere to fucking go. I know you don't have much money left, either. You playing yourself right now. So your best bet is to tell me what the fuck I want to know. Funny thing is, I went by the house to check on and talk to you, but as I pull up I see police cars and the ambulance. When I was allowed in MY fucking house I come across Trey and find out that your ass was rushed to the hospital for almost overdosing. Now I don't care about the drugs. I've known about that shit for a while now. You gave yourself the boot, Jalysa. Now you know if I saw Trey then I got some answers from his ass. So we can do this the easy way or the hard way. Your choice." I said.

She sat there looking like a deer caught in headlights. "Look, I was getting tired of you doing me wrong, so I made some decisions of my own. Now I'm damn near strung out and assed out. I know you killed Trey. I haven't been able to get in touch with him since I've been able to do anything in here. Yes, I've been talking to the boys, and I regret ever crossing you and your brothers." She said even more sadly. I stood there shaking my head.

"I haven't done anything to you for you to try to take away from my family and I. Fucking up my shit would've been more justifiable than anything else. But for you to put my life on the line is fucked up. Even though I know you didn't tell me everything, I want you out my fucking house anyway. The day your ass gets out of here, you better find a way to get the

141

fuck up out my house too. I let your ass get away with a lot of shit. It ends today. And for the last time there will never be an us again. And whoever your friend was, I'm sure you missed out on a good friend. To put up with you is enough. I'm giving you a week to get your shit out my house when you're released. Try me. And if you do anything else it won't end so great for you. You just might end up like Trey, and I never said what happened to him." I said turning to leave.

She didn't even let me get anywhere before she opened her mouth. "How are you going to do me like this? After all I've done for you, you're just going to throw it all away. I'm sorry, ok? I didn't mean anything I've ever done. I just wanted more from you. I deserve everything any hustler's wife gets." She screamed. I turned back around.

"See that's your problem. You're not a hustler's wife nor will you ever be one. You broke the main hustler's wife code: Don't snitch or turn on your man." I said walking away and leaving out. I could hear her calling my name, but I kept it moving.

She really thought she could get over on me. She hadn't seen the other side that I possessed, and I tried to keep it away from her, but she had been pushing my buttons since before we broke up. I will be keeping an eye out for her to see what slick shit she thingk she's going to try.

****

India

After seeing and talking to J, I headed to the store to grab some food for my room. I hailed a cab and made my way to the nearest store. I didn't want to have to haul a lot to the room from a cab, so I just grabbed a few things. It didn't take me long to get what I needed. On the way back to the hotel, I felt like I was being followed, but every time I looked around I didn't see anything out the ordinary anyone. But the feeling never went away. When we got to the hotel I paid the driver, grabbed my bags, and quickly made my way to my room. When I got to my door and was about to put the key in, a hand appeared out of nowhere touching mine.

"Take your ass inside and don't you say a word. If you scream I swear I'll shoot your ass." I recognized that voice from anywhere. As soon as I got the door open, Tank pushed me through the door. I almost fell, but I caught myself.

"Put that shit up and then sit the fuck down. Now yesterday your ass thought you was cute talking all that shit. But today it's not happening." He said pushing me in the kitchen.

I rolled my eyes and went ahead and put the stuff away. But as I was doing that, I got my phone out my purse and called Granmie. I heard her answerr , but I couldn't say anything. I tried to send her a text but I heard him coming. I put my phone down somewhere he couldn't see it, again. I knew the moment she heard his voice she would know why I called.

"What the fuck is taking you so damn long to put the shit away. I know you didn't grab that much shit since I was watching you." He said. I turned and looked at him.

"I knew I was being followed. Why the fuck won't you leave me the fuck alone? I don't want shit to do with you anymore, especially finding out that you've been in contact with that bitch Jalysa." I said standing up and crossing my arms across my chest.

The look he gave me would've scared me months ago, but I stood there not wavering not one bit. "Bitch, I ought to knock you the fuck out. How dare you ask me anything. Who gives a fuck about how I know Jalysa and why? What's important is your ass coming the fuck back home." He said getting in my face.

"Not going to happen." I said. "Listen here—" He started.

"No you listen here. The day you took my son away from me was the day I was done with you. I told you I'm not that young ass naïve girl anymore. I'm not going to be your punching bag emotionally, verbally, or physically anymore. I'm done with you. I fucking deserve better. I deserve to be treated like the good female that I am. You no longer have any control over me.." I was saying with my finger in his face but then there was a knock on the door. We looked at each other.

I had confusion written all over my face. "If you called security on me, I swear." He said pointing his finger at me.

"Ain't nobody scared of you." I said pushing him out my way. When I got to the door and looked through the peephole my whole mouth dropped. Now how in the hell did J find me. I opened the door soon as Tank brought his ass out the kitchen.

"What the fuck is taking you so fucking long to find out who it is?" He asked when he appeared. I looked at J who was looking at Tank weirdly. When Tank finally looked at J a smirk appeared on his face. I looked back and forth at them.

"Ummmm am I missing something here? Do ya'll know each other or something?" I asked. Neither said anything.

I stood there for a couple minutes waiting for either of them to say anything, but they didn't. They just stared at each other. I started waving my hands in J's face. Without looking at me he asked, "Am I interrupting something?"

"No, you're not. He was actually leaving." I said turning to look at Tank.

"No the fuck I wasn't and I'm glad I'm not. How do you know this fuck nigga?" He said pointing to J. I turned and looked at J.

"Hold up. Ya'll actually know each other?" I asked.

"Unfortunately." J said. "How do you know him?" J asked finally looking at me.

"He's the situation I told you about that I had in Cali." I said not caring that Tank could hear what I was saying.

"Oh really?" J asked with an eyebrow raised.

"I can only imagine what that situation actually was. Knowing that nigga nothing has changed. Still have a hand problem, Robert?" He said looking at Tank.

"Robert? Who the hell is Robert?" I asked looking between them again.

J started laughing. "I see you're still at your old tricks. Still lying to the ladies, huh?" J asked.

Tank walked over to us so quick. He pushed me out the way so quick that I didn't know what happened next. I fell back and hit my head on the table that was by the door. Everything went black. I woke up on the couch. I sat up looking around trying to figure out what the fuck was going on. It was dark in the room. I heard a noise and stood up, but that wasn't such a good idea. My head started pounding immediately. I grabbed the back of my head and felt a knot.

"The fuck happened to me? How did I end up on the couch?" I asked myself looking around. As soon as the words left my mouth my memory started coming back.

"I would sit down if I were you." I heard. I turned to see J coming in the room.

"What are you doing here? Where did Tank go? What the hell is going on?" I asked.

He started walking towards me. I started moving backwards. "Don't come near me." I said with my hands out in front of me. He stopped walking and put his hands up.

"Fair enough. I just ask that you hear me out." He said looking at me like he did in the park.

"Fine. I guess. Now start talking." I told him.

"Can you at least sit down. I'm harmless." He said sitting on the couch. I was standing near the desk that was in the room.

"I'll sit here. Now talk." I said pulling the chair out and sitting down. He looked down and then took a deep breath.

"Everything I told you at the park was the total truth. Like anyone else I just didn't go into depth about what really went on in my world. Tank, as you may know him as, is from California but use to visit his grandmother here every summer for a few years gowing up. His grandmother used to stay around my way. So I obviously knew him, and we used to hang out. We were actually good friends until we both started selling drugs. That's when things took a turn for the worse. He joined the wrong team, and I obviously joined the right team. He got jealous and has had it out for me ever since. Some crazy things have been happening a lot lately, and since he's here I'm beginning to believe that he's the reason behind it all. I wouldn't put it past him." He said finally looking up at me.

I started shaking my head. "Impossible. There's no way he used to deal drugs. I don't believe it." I said.

"How well do you know him?" He asked me.

"We use to date. Wait. What the hell happened earlier? Where did he go? And I know him well enough." I said.

"When he pushed you out the way, you hit your head and passed out. We ended up fighting, and I whipped his ass like I used to back in the day. He got mad and took off, but not before saying he would be back and it wasn't the end of things." He told me. I couldn't believe what I was hearing.

"I can't believe any of this. Why should I believe anything you're saying?" I asked standing up folding my arms.

"Because for one I have no reason to lie, and two because I know you have more than enough reasons to believe he's no good. You don't know him like I know him." He said standing up himself.

"What's that supposed to mean?" I asked.

"Has he ever laid his hands on you?" He asked. I looked down.

"You're not the first and you won't be the last. Did you end up pregnant, and he made you lose your baby?" He asked.

My head shot up quick. He started nodding his head. "I'm sorry." He said.

My hand shot to my mouth, and I started crying. I started shaking my head like I was fucking crazy. "No. No. No. This can't be. Why are you still here?" I asked once I calmed myself down. "Oh my god. Granmie." I said running to the kitchen to find my phone. I found it and saw that she hung up. I turned around, and he was standing right there. I quickly backed up.

"Are you ok?" He asked. I called Granmie back.

"Oh my God. Thank God you're ok. I've been sitting here praying ever since I didn't hear your voice anymore. What the hell happened?" She asked.

"You're not going to believe this, Granmie. So I go to the hospital to visit that girl and that didn't end well. I'll tell you about that later." I said looking at J. He nodded his head and walked away.

"Ok so I go to the store to grab a few things to eat for the room, and when I get to the door Tank pops up. So he pushes me inside and while I'm telling his ass off, as you could hear, there was a knock at the door. The guy I told you I met was at the damn door. So you know I'm like oh shit this isn't going to end well. So I open the door and low and behold these niggas know each other, Granmie. Next thing I know I wake up on the damn couch with a knot on the back of my head from being pushed out the way, so they could fight. And then the guy I met is still here then I thought about you." I said all in one breath.

"Girl stop. You lying. Now I only heard but so much. Once I stopped hearing your voice, I heard a commotion and was about to call the police. I told myself if I didn't hear from you before the night was over, I was definitely calling their asses. Now is the guy fine?" She said.

"Granmie." I said palming my forehead.

"Oh, baby, I'm just saying. But are you ok?" She asked.

"Yes, Granmie, I'm good. The guy and I are talking, and I'm finding some things out that I'm going to have to talk to you about on the next call." I said.

She started laughing. "What's funny?" I asked.

"Girl, you haven't ever had this much going on even when you was in Cali. Shit this is better than them damn reality shows and my stories put together." She said all excited.

"Oh my goodness, Granmie. Bye. I love you." I said.

"Love you too, baby. Make sure you get all the tea." She said and hung up.

I just shook my head. I walked back in the living room to find J on his phone. I sat back down and waited for him to get off the phone. About a minute or so later, he finally hung up.

"I had to tell my brothers what happened and that nigga was in town. So I heard you talking to your grandmother. Are ya'll pretty close?" He said.

"Yea we're very close. She's all I have left in the world. Now back to you and Tank." I said.

"Ok let's get one thing straight. I don't know where that nigga got the name Tank from, but his name is Robert. He's not as hard as he comes off to be. He's always used his hands to make up for his weakness." J said.

I sat there looking at him not believing what I was hearing about Tank. After all this time he wasn't who he claimed or portrayed to be.

"One question." I said.

150

"Shoot. What's that?" He asked sliding to the edge of the couch.

"Why did you come here?" I asked curiously.

"I wanted to see you again. I couldn't wait until tomorrow for dinner." He said. I nodded my head.

"One more thing. Can you get me a gun and teach me how to shoot?" I asked. He looked at me like I was crazy.

"Don't ask any questions. Just tell me yes or no. I'll get it with or without you." I said matter- of- factly. He looked at me.

"Tell me why first." He said folding his hands together.

"I need protection from that lunatic for one, and I've always wanted to learn how to shoot anyway. On top of that I know that things just got crazy. By what you said, he's definitely coming back and I need to be prepared. I promised myself, Granmie, and my unborn son that he would never lay another hand on me again." I said looking at him with the most serious look ever.

"Ok." He said.

Chapter 10

Jace

After leaving the hospital I couldn't get India off my mind. I wanted to see her again, so I found my way towards the Sheraton downtown. I had to flirt and pay the desk service agent to get India's room number. I knew I could've just called and ask her, but I wanted to surprise her. When I got there I heard her talking then I heard a man's voice, and I was skeptical to even knock on the door at that point. I hoped she wasn't trying to play me. I didn't get that vibe from her. When she answered the door, I was happy to see her until a familiar fucking face popped up. Now I was thrown for a loop. I was standing there wondering how in the hell could she possibly know Robert's ass. When all that shit popped off and I saw India hit her head, I beat his ass real quick so I could check on her. After he took off, I picked her up and laid her on the couch. I was hoping she wouldn't be out for too long, but her ass was out for damn near three hours. I told her most of what I could tell her. She would have to find the rest out on her own.

See many knew who he wais but didn't actually know him. My brothers and I knew the real him. He is one fake ass dude, and I hope the truth about him comes out sooner rather than later. When I asked her if she was pregnant and did he make her lose the baby, I felt bad for her. He had done that so much over the years that he should be put the fuck away. His situation was pretty fucked up, but like I said, she was going to have to find all that out on her own. When she got on the phone with her grandmother, I'm not going to lie, I was ear hustling like hell, but I eventually walked away brcause of the look she gave me. I figured I could call my brothers to tell them what the fuck was going on while I waited on her to finish up on the phone. I called Jackson up first.

"What's good, Bruh?" He answered. I ran my hand down my face.

"Man, you're not going to believe what the fuck happened in the past couple of hours." I said.

"Oh shit. What happened?" He asked.

"Ok so first I go see Jalysa and that bitch tried to play dumb, but I had something for that ass. I told her pack her shit and get the fuck out my house when she was released. Mainly because of what she did or tried to do. But before all that happened I ran into shorty, I been telling you and June about, in front of the hospital. So after seeing Jalysa's bum ass, I figured I'd run up on shorty where she staying at. I'll get into that later. So I get here and guess who the fuck is in her room with her?" I say.

"Ahhh, nigga, don't nobody have time to be guessing. Shit who, nigga?" He asked.

"A nigga we haven't seen or heard from in a long ass fucking time. That nigga Robert." I said and waited for his reply.

"Nigga, you lying. That weak motherfucker? Wait. How in the blue fucking hell do shorty and him know each other?" He asked.

"Now you asking the right fucking questions. So she tells me they used to fucking date." I said. I heard thatis nigga choking.

"You a fucking lie, yo. Hell no. Fuck no. Ain't no way." He said.

"My nigga, what makes it bad is that he's still up to his old ways. He still putting his hands on females and making them lose their baby. Bruh, she even knew what she was having, a boy, yo." I said.

"Damn yo. That's fucking crazy. Wait. Does shorty even know what and who the fuck she dealing with?" He asked.

"Not at all, my nigga, and I can't be the one to tell her. She already didn't believe the little shit that I did tell her." I told him. I could tell he was sitting there shaking his head.

"Yo that's fucking wild, my nigga. She gotta know, though. She just can't not know. But if we know that nigga like we do, then we know that he's coming back. Aye, do you think he's the one that's been doing this shit to us?" He asked.

"I swear I was thinking the same fucking thing. I don't know how long he's been in town, but if he's been here as long as all this shit been going on then it's a strong fucking possibility. Did June ever get back to you about what he found in that truck?" I asked.

"I feel you. We need to find that shit out ASAP. Naw I've been waiting on his call about that one my damn self. We might need to meet up on that one. If he hits me up, I'll let you know the deal." He said.

After he finished talking India came back in the room. "Aye, bruh, let me hit you back." I said.

"Love." He said.

"Love." I said hanging up.

India sat there patiently waiting for me to finish my phone call. We finished up our conversation, which I'm sure she had a lot more questions to ask. Shit I would if I was her. When she asked me to get her a gun, I was slightly confused but I definitely understood her reasoning. Women should always be protected and feel protected if they don't have a man to do so. I agreed to help her. Hell, to stay near her I probably would agree to anything sh says or asks for. We said we would set up a time and place to practice after our dinner tomorrow. We talked a little while longer before she decided to go to bed, because she was getting a headache and was becoming restless.

We said our goodbyes and I made my way out, but not before getting a hug from her. Something about touching and holding her just makes me feel good. As I was walking away from her door, after making sure she locked up good, my phone rang. I pulled it out and saw that it was June.

"What's good?" I answer.

"My house. Now nigga." He said and hung up.

I wasted no time making my way to my car and then to his house. It was very seldom we met up at his house, so I knew this shit couldn't have be good. When I finally got there, because this nigga liked to be ducked the fuck off in never ever find land, I saw that Jackson was already there. I parked, hopped out, and made my way to the front door which opened immediately.

"Bring your ass in here, nigga." June said when he opened the door. I walked inside and followed his ass to his office. We got inside and Jackson was in there with a drink in his hand.

"You might want to grab you a drink yourself, nigga." June said. I looked between him and Jackson.

"Naw tell me what's going on first." I said taking a seat.

"Suit yourself then, nigga. Ok first sorry it took me so long to get to ya'll about what was in the truck. I had to get me some pussy to keep me calm. I know, so don't say shit. We all good and that's all that matters. Anyway the shit I found out is fucking crazy. So the nigga's plan was throughout the whole truck and shit. I even grabbed his cell phone and went through his records. It's that nigga Robert we grew up with. He's behind all of this." June said looking at us both. Jackson and I looked at each other and smirked.

"Ok I saw that shit. What am I missing?" June asked leaning back in his chair.

I looked at him and smiled. "I had a run in with his ass earlier today. Coincidentally this nigga and the shorty I've been telling you about used to date back in Cali." I said waiting for his response.

"Fuck out of here. Impossible. There's no fucking way. Does she know?" He said. I just shook my head.

"Damn shorty caught the fuck up then." He said. "Right." Jackson and I said together.

"Ok I'm going to show you some shit that you just might not be prepared for, but you gotta see this." June slid me some pictures.

I looked at him and Jackson, and the look on their faces weren't good. I started flipping through the pictures, and I was getting madder the more I looked. I threw the pictures down and made myself a drink. I was ready to kill something. I was seeing red.

****

India

When J left I was too damn tired and my head was hurting like hell. I took a Tylenol and ran me a hot bath. I soaked in the tub for so damn long that I fell asleep. When I woke up the bubbles were gone, the water was cold, and I was wrinkled as hell. I finished washing myself up and got in the bed. It felt so damn good being in that bed. I slept so good. I woke up and felt so much better. I was ready to take on my day.

I was even more excited that I would finally learn how to shoot a gun. I had been wanting to do so since I left Tank. I still couldn't get over the things J told me about him. I wasn't really sure what to believe. I just met J, but I didn't see why he had much reason to lie about knowing somebody he said he grew up with. On top of that, I felt like there was more to the story that he didn't tell me. I couldan't wait to talk to Tank again. I decided to call Granmie before I did anything else.

"Hey baby. How you feeling today?" She asked when she answered.

"Hey, Granmie. I'm feeling much better. So you know I have the tea. You ready?" I said smiling.

"Girl stop. Let me go refill my glass real quick. I gotta hear this one." She said. I heard her moving in the background.

"OK, baby. Go ahead." She said.

"Ok, so I went to visit Jalysa at the hospital and the chick had the nerve to jump bad and talk a lot of shit. I did slap her ass twice though, and like usual, she didn't do a damn thing." I said.

"I've told you for years to watch out for that girl. She's a sneaky one. But go ahead." She egged on.

"And I should've listened to you. So I found out that her ass has been in contact with Tank. And somehow Tank has my new number and gave it to her. I told her ass off and left the hell out. I called Mama Joyce to tell her what was going on. She wasn't even tripping off Jalysa. I don't know what happened to my friend, but something has truly changed in her." I said shaking my head.

"No, baby, you were just too blind to see the real her. Her ways were always there. Anybody could feel and see the jealousy radiating off of her. I don't know how you stayed friends with her for so long. Something has always been up with her, but I could never put a finger on it." She said.

I stood there listening to her and wondered my damn self what the hell was wrong with me. "You're right, Granmie." I said.

"You damn right I'm right." She declared. I could hear the smile in her voice which caused me to laugh.

"Anyways, crazy lady, so when the guy was here last night he told me a few things about Tank." I said

"What the fuck else could possibly be wrong with his psycho ass?" She asked.

"I can tell there's more to the story than J said. But apparently Tank has been had a hand problem. Not only that, he purposely gets females pregnant and then makes them lose it. Oh and he used to sell drugs too. Oh and his real name is Robert." I told her. I could hear her spit out her drink.

"Girl, that was the end of my drink and you done made me spit it out." She said laughing.

I started laughing myself. "That nigga name is Robert? Oh hell naw. Something is up with his ass. I guarantee it. How well did that young man say he knew Robert?" She said putting emphasis on his name.

"They basically grew up together. He would come visit his grandmother every summer until they both decided to take the path of selling drugs. Something about they chose different teams, and Tank's team wasn't doing what J's team was, so that's when shit got started between the two." I told her.

"Well damn. Ain't that some shit. I should've refilled my glass, because that was a lot of got damn tea. Hunny, your ass flew into drama while trying to leave some. I hope psycho doesn't come back but I'm sure he is." She said.

"Oh I know he is, and I'm going to make sure I'm prepared for his ass from here on out. I'm going to learn how to shoot a gun and buy me one." I said matter- of- factly.

"Well it's about damn time. I told you to do that the moment you told me he put his hands on you, and you didn't want to leave his ass. You should've been did that, but like they say, "Better late than never." She said.

"I hear you, Granmie. Well I gotta go. I'll call you tomorrow. I have a date tonight with J." I said.

"Ok baby. Oh wait. Have you found a place for your salon yet?" She asked.

"No ma'am. Hell I haven't even looked for one yet, but I will soon enough. I promise." I said.

"Good. I want you to be living your dreams before I leave this earth, child." She said.

"Don't talk like that, Granmie." I said.

I hated when she talked like that. "Child please. We all gon' die one day. You know I'm old. It's going to happen. I don't know when and I don't know how, but it's going to happen. I just hope to live to see the smile on your face when you tell me you finally opened your shop." She said. "I'm sure your ass is over there crying and shit. Let me get my ass off this phone before you turn this shit into more than what it is. I love you, baby. Talk to you later." She said and hung up.

I couldn't even say anything. She was right I was crying. Every time she talked like that it made me emotional. She really is the only person I had left and if she left me then I would have nobody. And I didn't want that. I knew I was being selfish, but who didn't have that one person they didn't want to leave this earth, ever. After getting myself together, I made me something to eat and got dressed. I headed out the hotel only to run smack dab into Tank.

"You thought I wasn't going to come back? Let's go." He said yanking me by my arm. I pulled away just as fast as he grabbed me.

"I'm not going nowhere with you, Robert. You have some explaining to do." I said crossing my arms and mugging him.

"I don't have to explain shit to you." He said through gritted teeth.

"Like hell you don't. Why haven't you ever told me about your past? What are you hiding?" I asked through squinted eyes. I really wanted to know.

"I'm not telling you shit." He said.

"Well I'm not going nowhere with you. Hell, you somehow got in contact with the only person I had here and you fucking found me. Now your ass won't leave me the hell alone. I've never done anything to your ass. The least you can do is tell me why." I said looking at him.

"I don't know what the fuck your issue is, but you better get it together quick and in a hurry." He said.

"Look. I done told you, I'm done with your ass. You can't control me any damn more." I said.

"Listen to what she said, bruh." A voice said coming ftom out of nowhere.

I turned around to see J standing there. "What are you doing here?" I asked.

"Yea, nigga, the fuck are you doing here? This is my bitch." Tank asked from behind me.

"Nigga, don't get your ass beat again. Didn't she say she was done with you." J said.

"I'm not anybody's bitch." I said getting in Tank's face.

"Yea nigga. You know you don't want these problems. I'll air your ass out. So what's up?" Some other guy came out of nowhere and said.

I looked at him then J and could see the resemblance but also the differences. I could tell that he was a good couple of years younger than J.

"Hi, beautiful. I'm June. Jace's youngest brother." He said sticking his hand out.

"Did you just say Jace?" I asked. "Your name is Jace?" I asked turning to J and pointing to him.

"Yea." He said.

"Why?" He asked.

"Do you know a Jalysa?" I asked. "Yea that's my ex-girlfriend I told you about. Why?" He said.

"That's the friend I've been talking about this whole time. How could you have not known it was me?" I said.

"Oh Shit. This shit is about to get real." June said.

Then out of nowhere another guy came walking up. "What I miss?" He asked.

He looked like Jace too, but just like June I could see the differences. He looked younger than Jace but older than June.

"Hi, sweetheart. I'm Jackson. The nice one. It's good to finally meet you. I thought this nigga was lying about you, but he damn sure wasn't. Oh shit it's Robert's bitch ass. Emphasis on bitch." He said looking at Tank.

"So wait a minute ya'll know my ex- boyfriend and my ex best friend? This world is too fucking small." I said shaking my head.

"On behalf of my brothers and I, we want to apologize for you having to go through unnecessary bullshit this bullshitting ass nigga. He never knew any better since no one taught him how to be a MAN." June said with his hand over his heart putting emphasis on the word man.

Jackson and Jace both started shaking their heads. The next thing I know I was being pushed out the way; but I ended up behind Jace this time instead of falling somewhere.

"What the...." I started saying when I looked around his tall ass to see that Tank had pulled a gun out in broad fucking daylight.

"Tank, what are you doing?" I asked grabbing Jace's shirt.

"This nigga isn't stupid." June said reaching in his pocket.

"Naw, nigga, you know better. Not here." Jace said putting his hand on June's stopping him from going in the back of his pants.

"Naw, you know I don't care about that shit. He wanna be tough let his ass ride with the big boys. So what's up, nigga?" June said still going in the back of his pants and pulling out his gun.

Tank was heated. "I'm so sick of you niggas. Ya'll always thought ya'll was better than everybody." He said through gritted teeth.

"Nigga, now you know you lying. We always welcomed you to our side, but you thought you knew everything and stayed with them fuck ass niggas. Now you trying to take over our shit, but getting niggas killed left and right. You know you fucked with the wrong ones, right?" June said shooting Tank right in his legs.

"Man, get this fuck nigga the fuck up out of here. We about to handle this shit right now." Jace said. Then out of nowhere two more guys came, picked Tank up, and walked off with him.

Jace turned to me and put his hands on my shoulder. He looked me dead in the eyes. "Are you ready to find out the truth?" He asked. All I could do was nod my head. I needed to know the truth. He nodded in return.

"Let's go." He said grabbing my hand and pulling me towards his car. We all got in separate vehicles and took off. I didn't know how long we were driving, but I woke up as soon as we stopped.

"Where are we?" I asked looking around rubbing my eyes.

"We're at one of our spots. It's about to get crazy, so are you sure you want to know the truth?" He asked me.

"Yes. I want to know the truth." I said standing by my decision.

He got out the car and came and opened the door for me to get out. He put his hand out, and I grabbed it to get out. We walked inside and they already had Tank sitting in a chair. There was a bunch of tools and shit lying around. I looked at Jace and swallowed loudly. He looked at me and squeezed my hand for reassurance. We walked up on Tank, and he didn't look happy at all.

"Ok now you can finally tell the truth Robert. She deserves the right to know it all." Jackson said.

"Fuck you. Fuck her, and fuck all of ya'll. I'm so sick of ya'll. Ya'll don't know what the fuck I went through growing up." He said looking off.

"So tell me. I think I have the right to know why you treated me the way you did. I did nothing to you to get the treatment I received." I said walking up.

"You or any other bitch I've dealt with doesn't deserve any fucking thing from me." He said. I walked closer to him and punched him in his face.

"Damn that felt good." I said.

"Touch her. I fucking dare you." Jace said walking closer.

"Now fucking talk or we will talk for you." Jace said looking at Tank with his arms folded. If looks could kill Jace and his brothers would be dead.

Chapter 11

Jace

The drink I had calmed me down, so it made it a little easier to look through the rest of them pictures. This was a small fucking world. I couldn't believe the shit I was looking at. June handed pictures of Robert and Jalysa together. But that wasn't the bad part. The bad part was finding out that Jalysa used to be a man, and her and Robert was fucking around behind India's and my backs. I damn near threw up flipping through the pictures seeing them naked and shit. Trey told us there was some shit we would find out that we weren't ready for. I was ready to murder some damn body.

"Bruh, I'm sorry." June said.

"Don't say shit to me, man." I got up and walked out the office and house without another word.

I drove home so damn quick. I wanted to go to hospital and kill that bitch or whatever the fuck it was, but I had something better than that. That bitch was going to wish it never fucked with me. I had to tell India who and what she was dealing with. But I had a feeling that Robert's ass was going to pop up on India, and I was going to make sure I was there when he did. If he gets wrong then things won't end easy for his ass.

I was glad I went with my gut feeling, because low and behold that nigga was there trying to get her to do something she didn't want to. And just like I knew he would he wanted to jump bad. I think somebody forgot to tell him that if you pull a gun on som you better use it. June's crazy ass shot him in his legs. I called June and Jackson for them to meet me at the hotel, and I was glad that I did. Hell, I was happy that Tommy and Shawn's asses was near too, because I wasn't touching his bitch ass unless I was laying hands on him again. And he didn't want that at the moment.

I knew taking India to the spot was going to be a little hard on her, but she had to know the truth. I could tell that she was nervous and uncomfortable as hell. She started asking questions, but he wasn't budging. When I told him he better talk or I will, I saw a look come over him. He was scared shitless. Just the way I liked them to be when they we're in the hot seat. He must've grown some balls, or he just didn't want to look like the bitch he was in front of India.

"Ok. That's fine. You don't have to say shit. I'll do you one better." I said going over to a table and picking up a manila envelope. I walked back over to India and handed it to her.

"What's this?" She asked me.

"The truth." June said.

I watched India's face as she opened the envelope. She took one last look at me before pulling the pictures out. One by one she looked at the pictures and the expression on her face was as expected, not happy at all. As soon as she finished looking through the pictures she threw the pictures and threw up.

"Tell me this isn't true?" She asked looking at me. "I'm afraid it is." I said.

"How did you find out?" She asked holding her hand up to her chest and mouth.

"Remember how I told you that I felt he was behind some of the shit that was happening to my crew lately?" I asked her. She nodded.

"Well it is him. One night we were shot at at in our club and one of the shooters survived. We were followed and they waited until we left to ambush us, but we ended up getting them first. June stayed behind to look through the truck to see what he could find, and this is what he found. Trust me I'm just as surprised as you are. I was fucking the bitch for seven damn years. Not only was it a fucking man, but she also been snitching on me." I said.

"I'm going to kill that bitch." India yelled. "Wait. So you were the one she was talking about then. Wow." She said.

I looked at her wondering what she was talking about. "What you talking about?" I asked.

"The day we saw each other at the park, I had left the house because I caught the girl passed out from doing lines of coke. I couldn't take the shit. I came back to hear her talking to somebody about if you find out it's them that you're going to kill them. I walked in on her and this dude I had seen before, because him and his girl came to the house about him cheating on her with Jay. Now I don't know if he knew she was a man, but they had been messing around for a long time. That was the day I left her ass where she was at and went to the hotel. Now that explains how they know each other, but then again it doesn't. I've known that bitch for a long fucking time, since we were teenagers. I don't know how I didn't know she knew him. But they obviously belong together. I got something for her ass, though. I wanna kill the bitch myself. As a matter- of fucking fact somebody give me a gun right now. I don't need to hear shit else this faggot ass nigga has to say." She said holding her hand out.

"Fuck you. You don't know what I've been through. I hated coming here for the summers. My grandmother use to rape me every fucking day." Robert said.

"So the fuck what. You should've gotten counseling. So you take your gay ass shit out on fucking females who did nothing to deserve it. I lost my child because of your faggot ass. Where is the fucking gun?" She screamed.

June's crazy ass actually handed her a gun. The damn thing wasn't in her hand a damn second before she unloaded the shit into his whole body. I mean she lit that nigga up like the Fourth of fucking July.

"Well you don't need no damn target practice. Shit your ass doesn't even need a gun. Somebody make you mad and your ass will unload a clip on them." I said trying to lighten the mood.

"Shit, nigga, you better not ever make her ass mad. But shit, I like her ass though. Short, sexy, cute and can work a fucking gun. My kind of girl. If he ever fucks up just know I'm here for you." June said laughing. I pushed his ass.

She smiled and then looked at me. "Thank you." She said.

"Why are you thanking me?" I asked.

"For helping me get rid of a burden that I've been carrying around since I met his ass. I don't know how I missed all this shit. That shit was fucking sickening to see. So what are we going to do about Jalysa?" She asked.

"Don't you worry about that. I've got that taken care of. As a matter- of- fact are we still on for tonight?" I asked.

As always the clean up crew came walking their asses inside, but stopped when they saw India. "Damn." I heard one of them say.

"Naw. She's mine, nigga." I said wrapping my arms around her shoulders and walking her towards the door.

"My bad. She is bad, though." Another said. "Damn ya'll niggas actually do talk. But it's a good thing we don't pay ya'll to talk." June said.

They didn't say anything else. They got straight to work. We walked outside. I turned to India.

"You didn't answer my question." I said.

"Yes. We're still on to go out." She said looking at her watch.

"Oh damn. I need to get ready, though. Can you drop me off at the hotel so I can prepare?" She asked.

"Oh shit this nigga here done finally found him an actual female and don't know how to act. Doing dates and shit. This nigga don't ever do dates." June said. I gave him the finger and a look that said watch it. He threw his hands up. "My bad. Too soon." He said smiling.

Jackson stood there laughing. I looked at him with the same look, but his ass wasn't paying my ass any attention. I opened the door for India and helped her in. I looked at my brothers and said, "I'll get up with ya'll later. Love."

"Love." They said together.

By the time I got in the car the clean up crew was coming out. Everybody hopped in their cars and went on their way. The ride was quiet for a bit.

"How did you not know?" She asked out of nowhere.

"How did you not know?" I asked back.

"I don't know. Honestly. I mean I guess I never paid attention to the signs. Come to think of it they were all there. She would never get dressed or undressed in front of me. Besides a hug she never really let anyone touch her. She wouldn't have certain conversations when it came to females. I mean she definitely did change over the years, but I didn't necessarily see her physically. I mean I'm still trying to figure out how the hell her and Tank even knew each other. Hell I wonder if she ever thought you or anybody would ever find out. What do you plan to do?" She said.

"I don't know how I didn't know. I mean her body looked and felt natural to me. We never actually talked about starting a family, so that definitely didn't help any. But I have a plan so don't you. even worry about it." I said as we pulled up to the hotel. "Look if you don't want to stay here anymore I have some property that hasn't been touched in a long time that you can live in. I think it could be up to your standards." I told her.

"Oh no. I couldn't. I don't have much money to pay rent or any other bills. Hell I barely had the money too stay here." She said shaking her head then putting it down.

"Don't worry about all that. Look, I know you need to get ready so let's talk about it over dinner. I'll see you in a few hours." I said getting out to open the door for her.

She got out and smiled at me. "Want me to walk you to your room?" I asked.

She shook her head. "No. You don't need to. Thank you though." She said smiling even brighter.

Damn she had a beautiful smile. She walked off, and I watched as she walked into the hotel. She had a beautiful body to go with that smile. I shook my head biting my lip. I was determined to get that girl. I hopped back in the car and made my way home.

****

India

Finding all that shit out about Jalysa and Tank made me want to kill his ass all over again and then find Jalysa's ass and kill her or him, whatever the fuck it was. Pissed was an understatement. Like how did I miss that shit. In my head I kept trying to figure out what Jace had planned for her ass. Shit I couldn't believe that I like my ex best friend's ex. That shit is crazy as hell to me. Finding out that J has been Jace all this time was fucking crazy. I mean I had never seen a picture of him nor had she told me what he looked like. And how the hell was it that we didn't get caught together in the club. Jalysa's ass was way dumber than I thought.

When I got in my room, I leaned my back against the door once it closed. Today had been crazy as hell. After about five minutes of being like that I finally pushed off the door and made my way to the bathroom. I turned the water all the way hot to get the steam going in the bathroom. I wanted to be different tonight. Before going into the bathroom, I pulled out the dress and heels I wanted to wear. I hopped in the shower and stood under the water letting the water take away today's craziness. As soon as the water touched my hair I felt so much better. I washed myself up and hopped out. It wasn't until I hopped out the shower that I realized that for the first time since I lost my son, I didn't touch my stomach. I knew I would never forget my son, but I think I finally came to terms with what happened, because now I knew why it happened. I smiled knowing that I could finally stop blaming myself for what happened.

I walked out the bathroom with the towel wrapped around my body and head sitting down on the bed. I grabbed my lotion and put lotion on my body. I went back into the bathroom and unwrapped the towel on my head. I looked at my hair. I had so much of it. I hadn't worn it straight in so long, so I decided to do just that. I grabbed the blow dryer and began to blow dry my hair running my brush through it. It felt good running that heat through my hair. It took me about thirty minutes to finally get it how I wanted to. I left out the bathroom to grab my underclothes. I slid into the cutest black thong ever. I finally stood at the edge of the bed looking at the dress I chose to wear this evening. I picked up the black dress and pulled it over my head making sure I pulled my hair from inside of it. I made sure my boobs fit in it correctly. I chose a dress that I couldn't wear a bra with it, but my boobs were sitting in the dress oh so perfectly. I stood in the mirror to make sure my thong wasn't showing and that my ass looked good in the dress.

I spun around in the mirror making sure I looked ok. I went into the bathroom so that I could have some better light to do my make up. I really didn't care for it, so I just put on some eyeliner, mascara, and lipstick. I checked the time and it was almost time for Jace to come get me. I went to put my shoes on and as soon as I stepped in a shoe, there was a knock at the door. I hurried up and put my shoes on and ran to the door. I looked in the mirror by the door to make sure I looked ok. I calmed myself down and opened the door. Jace's back was facing me when I opened the door. When he finally turned around he was standing there with flowers in his hand. The look on his face made me blush.

"Wow." He said.

"I'm sorry. Damn. I mean Hi. You look beautiful." He said.

I smiled and said, "Thank you." I opened the door up some more.

"Come in. I just have to grab my clutch and I'll be ready." I said.

He walked inside and went straight to the living room and sat on the couch. I closed the door and ran to the bathroom to spray some of my favorite perfume from Estee Lauder on. I walked out and went to the kitchen to put the flowers in a vase. I went back in the room to grab my clutch. I walked out the room and into the living room.

"Ready." I said.

Jace stood up and looked at me up and down then licked his lips.

"Damn girl. You look absolutely amazing." He said. He shook his head.

"Let's get out of here before we don't make it to dinner." He said. I looked away trying not to laugh. I walked ahead of him to the door making sure I put a little extra in my walk but not too much. I opened the door and was about to move out the way to let him out when he attacked my lips out of nowhere.

"Mmmmmm." I moaned against his lips.

My arms went around his neck while his hands roamed my body starting with my hips. It was like Deja vu from the club. He pulled away and stared me in my eyes. I swear he read my whole life through my eyes in those few seconds. Not thinking straight, I grabbed his hand leading him to the bedroom. I closed the door behind us and pushed him towards the bed making him sit down. I opened his legs with mine and slowly pulled my dress over my head. I felt his hands on my body once the dress was up to my eyes so I couldn't see him. As soon as I had my dress over my head, he picked me up. I instantly wrapped my legs around his waist. He laid me on the bed slowly kissing me. I could taste the blunt he just smoked on his tongue that he stuck down my throat. He had one hand behind my head leaning on his elbow while he held my leg with the other.

He took his hand from behind my head and from my leg and slowly pulled my thong down. The further he pulled the lower he went down my body leaving a trail of kisses and sucking on my skin. He stopped at my breasts and used his tongue on them; that left me with goosebumps all over my skin. I started shaking from the chills he was giving me. He made his way down to my honey pot and took a nice whiff. I could see him close his eyes as if he was trying to remember what I smelled like. He opened my legs wider and went in with one strong lick. I don't even remember anything after besides me coming so hard and strong that I thought I was going to pass out.

He made his way back up my body. I don't even know how or even when he even pulled his pants off, but he entered me so smoothly that he was all the way in before I could even react. He started moving slow looking me in my eyes, but it was feeling so good that I arched my back and kept closing my eyes.

"Look at me while I do your body good." He said in my ear before kissing it, then biting it.

"Ahhhhhh." I called out opening my eyes looking at him. He pulled back and looked me in my eyes before kissing me again.

"Mmmmmm." I moaned again.

I didn't know what it was about his kisses, but they brought moans out of me every time his lips touched mine. I hadn't even seen his dick, but damn he had me wide open, literally. He was moving in and out of me, so smoothly that I didn't want him to stop or pull out. But he did and went back down to my honey pot licking me so good, that I came, again. I was ready to go to sleep at that point. He came up and turned me on my side. I turned he wanted me.

"Naw. I said look at me." He said.

I looked at him. Hell I never had anyone be so demanding, but be smooth with it that I had no choice but to listen to him. He grabbed my ass so tight I know he to had left a handprint. He lifted my leg and slid right back in. He put my leg on his shoulder and started kissing my leg while he rubbed my ass with one hand and my clit with the other.

"Fuck Jace." I called out. I tried to put my hand on his stomach, but he pushed my hand away.

"Damn girl." He said closing his eyes for a second and leaning his head back.

He leaned forward and started caressing my breasts. He was playing with my nipples and clit at the same time, and in no time I was coming just as hard as I did the first time.

"Shit." I called out. He tapped my ass.

"All fours, baby." He said leaning in even further to kiss me.

I tasted myself on his lips, and I licked all my juices off his lips. When he pulled away, I licked my lips and got on all fours. I started shaking my ass and looking back at him. He was standing there stroking his dick and biting his lip. I finally got a good look at his meat and damn was all I could think. It was so beautiful glistening with my juices.

"Keep going, ma. Don't stop." He said. I kept on shaking my ass.

I turned to look forward when I felt a sting on my ass. "I didn't tell you to stop looking at me." He said. I turned back around to look at him when he pulled me to the edge of the bed and slid his dick back in me.

"Fuck ma." He called out.

He grabbed my hips and started beating my shit up. I mean the bed was hitting the wall and everything. I tried my hardest not to fall and to keep my arch in my back, but baby was giving me the business. I was so into how it was feeling that I didn't even realize he slowed down. Then I felt his dick pulsating in me before he let out a low growl and gripped my hips so tight. He stayed like that for a minute before his body collapsed beside mine. It was at that moment I realized we didn't use a condom, and I wasn't on birth control anymore.

"Oh my god, we didn't use a condom." I said hopping up. Well I tried to. He pulled me back down.

"You're mine, baby. If it happens then I got you." He said kissing my neck.

Not even a minute later he fell asleep just the way he was. I laid there looking at him wondering how this was going to work when he used to be my ex best friend's man. The day she finds out it's going to be another war. I wasn't even worried about that at the moment, though. I'll handle it when the time came. Until then I was going to bask in this wonderful feeling I was having at the moment. I looked at Jace for a couple more minutes before sleep found me too.

Chapter 12

Jace

After dropping India off at the hotel, I went home and figured out what I was going to wear. While I was looking my phone rang. I looked at it and it was my brother June calling.

"Yea nigga." I answered.

"Aye man. Why you ain't tell me shorty was that damn fine. Bruh, I wish I saw her first. I would've been all on that. Hell, I thought she was a ghost for a second since we hadn't seen her yet. I honestly wasn't believing your ass for a minute." He said.

"Nigga, shut the hell up." I said laughing.

"Don't you fuck with my girl, nigga. She's mine." I told him.

"Man I know but just know I was serious when I told her that I'm always there for her when you fuck up. Shit I'll be whatever she needs me to be when you fuck up." He said.

"Nigga, get off my phone so that I can get ready for my date with her." I said.

"Oh shit. I forgot about that. Did you get everything set up?" He asked.

"Yea nigga. It's all set up." I said.

"Well alrighty then mister fucking romantic. I hope your ass gets some ass with this shit." He said.

"You know me better than that man." I said.

"Yea. Yea. Nigga, I hear you. I'ma let you go, Mr. Romance. I'll talk to your sucker ass later. Love." He said.

"Love." I replied hanging up.

I stood there shaking my head at my brother. He was a straight up fool. I couldan't wait until the day his ass ran into the right female that was going to have him hooked and going crazy. I was going to laugh so hard. I finally found my outfit, so I walked into my bathroom to take a shower. When I got in the shower, I started thinking about everything that happened in the past couple of days. I still couldn't believe the shit I found out. I was still trying to figure out how in the blue fucking hell I didn't know that bitch was a man. Now I had known all along about Robert's ass. What my brothers or anybody else didn't know was that Robert's ass tried to hit on me when we were young, and that was the first time I ever beat his ass. He knew not to fuck with me on that level ever again. I looked past his gayness and still remained friends with him.

I didn't have any issues with gay people as long as they kept that shit away from me. Hell, some of our employees at the clubs were gay. And they we're some damn good workers too. I don't discriminate, but shit keep it one hundred with me. But like I said, I got something for her ass. Hell, I remembered seeing Jalysa and India together, but I didn't put two and two together. I mean it wasn't like India said the name of the friend she was talking about. I did know one thing though, when Jalysa finds out that I've been dealing with India she's going to lose her fucking mind. But I couldn't worry about that. Hell, I didn't even care. She wasn't my problem any more. Hell, I needed to find out what her status was in the hospital, so I could start the process of getting her the fuck out my house.

I was in the shower so long from thinking about all that bullshit that the water got cold. I got out the shower quick and wrapped the towel around my body. The whole time I was getting dressed, I was thinking about India and how she handled that damn gun. I kind of got scared for a second. Anyone would think her ass done had some training before the way she shot that nigga up, but it could've just been the adrenaline rushing through her body. I knew one thing, I was not going to make her ass mad and especially when a gun is in her possession.

I'm not going to lie. I was actually happy to be going out with her. Getting some more alone time with her is going to be good. I hope our conversation is as good as it was at the park. When I got dressed, I made sure I smelled and looked good. I looked in the mirror before leaving I normally drove my Charger, but tonight I decided to bring out the Bentley. I liked to bring it out on special occasions.

I hopped in the car and made my way to the hotel, but I made a stop and grabbed her some flowers. I knew it was a little cheesy, but I didn't know a female who wouldn't want flowers. When I got to her door, I wanted the flowers to be a surprise, of course, so I turned my back towards the door to hid them instead of hiding them behind my back. When she opened the door and I saw her, I couldn't help but stare. She looked absolutely amazing. To keep my mouth from dropping, I had to lick and bite my lips. While I waited for her to grab her things, I had to pray to God that I kept my composure. That girl there was one bad ass female. As she walked in front of me towards the door, I couldn't help but stare at her ass. I mean the way that shit was swaying had me hypnotized. I damn near bumped into her when she got to the door. I couldn't help myself with kissing her. I needed to feel her lips against mine, so I kissed her. I knew I caught her off guard, but it didn't seem like she minded.

I felt up and down her body. And man that shit was soft like I remembered. I had to restrain myself from going any further with her, but damn was her body calling me. I didn't know what was going on in her head. When she grabbed my hand and lead me to the bedroom, I swear I was trying to fight the urge to follow her but she and my dick won. Shit who was I to deny a female of a good time. And when I say a good time, I mean a damn good time.

Her pussy felt just as good as she looked. I mean her body was truly amazing and her pussy was even better. I swear I could've stayed in it all day and night. That shit was so good it knocked me the fuck out. Now that had never happened to me before. When I woke up she was still sleep and boy the way she was sleeping was so beautiful. I guess I was tired, because when I checked my phone, I had mad missed calls from my brothers. I put my boxers on and headed out to the living room to call them back.

"Nigga, did you get lost or something?" June answered.

"I swear, nigga, if you tell me some stupid shit I swear I'll hang up on your ass, come find you, and kick your ass. Well try to at least. I know you didn't have me make sure shit was straight for you just to not show the fuck up. Bruh, where are you?" He rambled on.

"If you would shut the fuck up then I could tell you that we never made it out her room." I said.

He was quiet for a second. "Oh shit. My nigga finally got some ass. Well it's about got damn time. I just knew you was going to die old and lonely with some big ass balls. Bruh, I swear I could give her a kiss right now." He said all hyped and shit.

"Chill nigga. Don't get your ass beat now." I said.

"Oh shit. This nigga already overprotective over a chick that ain't even his. My nigga sprung already." He clowned.

"Fuck you, nigga. Are you done? You know I'm good so call your brother and let him know. Only call me if ya'll need me. I'm spending the day with her." I told him turning around to see her standing in the doorway. She had the sheet wrapped around her body, and her hair was some kind of wild, but it looked beautiful surrounding her face. June was talking, but I didn't hear a damn word he said. "Love." I said and hung the phone up.

I walked over to her and looked down at her. For me not to know much about her I felt like I knew her well. Her short ass was so beautiful in the mornings. She had a glow on her face, and it made her brown skin look even more radiant. She had to only be about 5'4". But it didn't matter I'd stoop as far down as she needed me to.

"Good morning." She said with a slight smile.

"Good morning." I replied.

She was about to say something, but once again I couldn't help myself so I kissed her with morning breath and all. When we pulled away from each other, I think our eyes mirrored each other's with passion. After a few moments of staring at each other she shied away. I grabbed her chin making her look at me again.

"You're mine." I told her again and meaning it.

"Yea ok. I know this is cliché to say but I've never done that before. Something just came over me, and I couldn't help myself." She said seriously.

"I believe you. And I'm serious, you're mine." I said letting her chin go.

"Look. I know we were supposed to have dinner. Now we're going to hang out all day. Just me and you. I already talked to my brother and told him to not disturb me unless it's important. Are you ok with that?" I said looking her in her eyes.

She smiled. "I would like that." She said.

"Ok well I'm hungry so let's order some breakfast and talk. You order whatever you want then we'll go from there." I said kissing her on her forehead and walking away.

"Ok." I heard from behind me.

I went into the bathroom and closed the door. I stood there smiling. I finally got her, and no I wasn't happy because I got the goods early, but because she was actually mine. I could feel it in my bones that she was the one. I couldn't wait to see how things go between us. I think my sisters would like her. Hell my brothers already like her. I got in the shower and just thought about all the what ifs.

****

India

When I said I was surprised at myself that's exactly what I meant. I wasn't lying when I said I had never done that before. I was standing there as he walked away wondering what he was really thinking about me. He said I was his but I didn't know for sure if he was serious or running game. I walked to the phone and sat down on the couch to think about what I wanted to order. I wasn't sure what he wanted, so I just went with my gut. I grabbed the phone and ordered us some eggs, bacon, sausage, French toast, fruit, home fries and orange juice. I hope he likes what I ordered, because if not his ass was just shit out of luck.

I was a little bummed that we didn't get to go to dinner last night, but I definitely enjoyed what we did do, though. I sat there smiling about what happened last night. I didn't realize how long I was sitting there until I heard a knock at the door. I snapped out of it, and then I heard a phone going off. It silenced then started ringing again. As soon as I got to the door, Jace came walking out in a towel wrapped around his brown skinned body, and I lost all train of thought.

"Is that the food, baby?" I heard but it didn't register.

I kept looking at his chiseled chest that had a tattoo on it. I mean the man was absolutely perfect when naked. I hated that he had to wear clothes. Now that I actually got to see his body in the light, I thought I had fallen in love just that damn quick.I've never seen a body so perfect. I snapped out of my trance when there was a knock again.

"Oh umm let me get that." I said turning towards the door.

"Who is it?" I called out.

"It's room service." I heard a female say.

When I opened the door, the door got pushed in, and I went flying back. I caught myself on the table by the door this time. It kind of felt like Deja vu again.

"What the fuck? Jace? India?" I heard. I looked up to see it was Jalysa. I looked at Jace who was standing there with a smirk on his face.

"How the fuck did you find out where I was staying?" I asked after getting myself together.

"You ok, baby?" Jace asked walking over to me.

"Baby?" Jalysa screamed.

"What the fuck is going on here? How the fuck do ya'll know each other?" She asked looking between us both.

"No, bitch, you're going to answer my question. How the fuck did you find out where I'm staying?" I asked getting in her face.

She backed down real quick. "I got released yesterday and happened to see Jace out, so I followed him and saw him coming here. I followed him to this room and then waited outside all night trying to see who he was here with. He never came out, so I decided to come knock on the door to find out for my damn self." She replied rolling her head and neck around.

"Bitch, get the fuck out my room before I beat your ass." I said pointing to the door. Not even a second later there was another knock at the door again.

"When I open this door you better be walking the fuck out of here, Jay, and I fucking mean it. Do not test me. I'm not in the mood for your fucking shenanigans today." I said starting to make my way to the door.

"You have a week to get the fuck out my house if not I'll drag your ass out my damn self. Now test me, because I've been wanting a reason to fuck your ass up." Jace said from behind me.

I knew what he was talking about, but she didn't. The look on her face was priceless. Her ass was scared fucking shitless.

As soon as I opened the door, her ass made a beeline out of it without another world with her scary ass. She almost knocked over the server who was about to walk in the room with our food. I really couldn't believe that bitch really tried me. Now I felt for her about finding out about me and Jace, but then again I didn't give a fuck. She knew what was good for her and got the hell on, though. I knew that wouldn't be the last time I saw her. And when I did I'll be ready for her or his ass. I looked at the waiter with apolegtic eyes.

"I'm sorry about that. Come in." I told the server.

After making sure everything was right, I tipped the guy, and he was on his way. When I turned back around Jace was standing over the food lifting up trays and nodding his head.

"Is that what you like? I wasn't sure so I just went with my gut." I said.

"It's perfect. It's actually all my favorites. So come over here and let's eat." He said smiling at me. I smiled back, but I was too happy on the inside knowing I got it right. I went and sat down at the table and we fixed our plates.

"So I know we're kind of doing things backwards but oh well. You have to start somewhere. How old are you?" He said before putting a mouthful of food in his mouth.

I looked up at him before speaking and smiled. "Don't you know you're not supposed to ask a lady her age?" I said sweetly. He chuckled covering his mouth.

After he chewed his food he said, "Yes I know, but I just have to make sure that I'm not robbing any cradles here." He said with a smile. The smile on my face went away quickly.

"I don't look that young. To answer your question, I'm 27 years old. How old are you, Mr. Jace?" I said smartly and rolling my eyes.

"Oh don't be mad. I'm just saying. Can't be too careful these days. You know ya'll women know how to fool people. I mean look at what Jalysa did." He said.

"Ah. Point taken." I said stuffing food in my mouth. After chewing I asked, "Well how old are you?" I asked because he didn't answer the first time.

"I'm 28." He said simply.

"And why don't you have a wife and kids yet?" I asked.

"Because I hadn't met you yet." He said smoothly looking at me ever so intensely.

It instantly got hot in there. I started fanning myself and then took a sip of my orange juice. I had to look somewhere else besides him because looking at him was going to make me even hotter.

"I'm not going to lie, and you may have never heard anything like this, but I'm the male version of a hopeless romantic. Anybody who knows me personally, and I mean really knows me, knows that's how I am. And the moment I saw you after you bumped into me, I knew I wanted you. Hell you didn't even know who I was and that's a first. My brothers thought you were somebody I made up, because they had yet to see you." He said laughing. I cracked a smile. "Now that we got that out the way. Tell me your dreams and aspirations." He told me.

I always get this far off look when I start talking about my passion. "I don't care how you feel about what I'm about to say, but this is something that I know I was born to do. I want to own a chain of hair salons. I love to do hair." I said smiling just thinking about the day I would open up my first shop.

"I'm glad you have a goal. Your hair is beautiful every time I see you, so I can only imagine what you can do with it and other women's hair." He said.

"Man, back home in Cali I was the go to girl for all the females in the area. Hell females from other areas were calling me up. I just can't wait to live out my passion. I've been doing hair for as long as I can remember." I said smiling.

"Wow. I can tell that you really have a passion for it. Well I have sisters who looks for a new hairdresser damn near every week. If you're as good as you say they will stick with you. Believe me." He said laughing.

"Oh we're meeting the family already?" I asked with a smirk on my face.

"Well I mean you're going to be my wife so you might as well." He said not smiling anymore.

Saved from that little serious moment, I heard my phone ringing. I went over to it and looked at it not recognizing the number.

"Hello?" I answer curiously.

"Hi, is this India?" A female said.

"This is she. Who is this?" I asked skeptically.

"I'm, um, calling from St. Agnes. You're the emergency contact for your grandmother. She had a heartache and stroke. She's in recovery, but I have to warn you that she's not the same." She said. I just dropped the phone and fell to the floor.

"Baby, are you ok?" I heard Jace ask, but I couldn't respond. He kept asking me until he realized I wasn't going to answer. I could even hear the lady on the phone saying "Hello." Jace picked up the phone and spoke with the person. I didn't even realize I was crying until I felt my tears hitting my hand.

The next thing I knew Jace was picking me up and holding me tight. "Baby, she's going to be ok. Let's pack you a bag to take on the airplane." He said.

"I don't have the money to go, but I have to be with her. She's all I have left." I said crying.

"Come on. Don't you worry about all that. Let's go see your grandmother. Go pack you a few things or we can go now." He said walking me to the bedroom. "Let me make some calls and we can go." He said kissing me on my forehead.

I sat down on the bed and just stared off into space. I didn't move not one inch. I didn't know how long I was just sitting there, but all I knew was Jace came back in the room and grabbed me by the hand pulling me up. I saw him moving around the room getting dressed and then finidng me something to put on.

" Put this on and let's go. Where's your keys and stuff?" He asked.

"It's by the door." I said solemnly putting the clothes on.

"Ok." He said walking me towards the door once he saw that I was dressed. He made sure to grab my phone, purse, and keys. We walked outside the hotel and waited for his car from the valet.

Chapter 13

Jace

When Jalysa showed up it took everything in me not to shoot her ass right then and there. I swear I was ready to square up with her like the nigga she really was. But I had to contain myself. I was happy that India got rid of her ass without having to actually lay hands on her even though it would've been nice to see if she could really fight. We were having a good conversation while eating until she got that phone call. I had to make some calls, because I knew that if we took a regular flight that we could possibly be waiting for a good while. I called my homey up to get the family's jet fueled up and ready to go. She told me her and her grandmother were real close and I knew how she was feeling at the moment. I damn near collapsed when I found out about my mother when I was young. I had to call my brothers to let them know what was going on.

"Yea bruh? You finally got the pussy, nigga?" June asked when he answered.

"I normally would joke around with you but right now I can't. My girl just got a call about her grandmother having a heartache and stroke, so we're about to fly out to Cali. Hold it down. You already know the deal. I'll be back as soon as possible." I told him.

"Damn bruh. That's crazy. Tell shorty we got her if she needs anything. Ya'll be safe and keep me posted and shit. I'll let Jackson know. Love." He said.

"Love." I replied hanging up.

That nigga may play around a lot, but when shit got real he knew when to be serious. I didn't have any doubt that my brothers would and could hold it down while I was gone. When I went to get India so that we could go, I began to feel even worse for her. The look on her face was as if she had already lost her grandmother. When we finally got my car and got it, I grabbed her hand and gave it a squeeze to reassure her that everything was going to be ok.

We got to the hanger in no time and was on our way to Cali within minutes of me talking to the pilots. By the time I made it to my seat India was knocked out. I guess that was a good thing, because I didn't want her to worry too much. I sat down and tried to enjoy the ride, but I knew once we landed that things weren't going to be good. I ended up falling asleep and was awaken by the stewardess shaking me.

"Jace, we're here, hun." She said.

I nodded my head as I looked over at India. She was slowly waking up. She sat up and yawned looking around. She had a look of relief on her face for a quick second before reality sunk in and her face saddened. I got up and walked over to her holding my hand out. After she took my hand and stood up I walked us up to the pilot who was waiting on us to exit the plane.

"I'll call you when we're ready to head back." I said giving him a handshake.

He nodded his head. We headed down the stairs and got into the SUV I had waiting for us. Still holding onto India's hand, I kissed it. She was looking out the window, but turned to me and gave me the best smile she could muster up, which wasn't much. Then she turned back to looking out the window again. I pulled my phone out sending a text to my brothers to let them know we landed.

I got responses back immediately telling me to keep them updated. The drive to the hospital was a little long and very quiet. When we pulled up India took a deep breath before getting out. We made our way inside to the front desk. We walked up to the receptionist desk.

"Yes, may I help you?" The receptionist asked without looking up.

"I'm looking for the room of Mai Brooks." India spoke up. The receptionist started typing.

About a minute later she said, "Room 618." She still hadn't looked up. Hell, at least we were acknowledged but damn.

We quickly made our way up to her grandmother's room. When we got there, India didn't waste any time walking inside. When I walked in, India was just standing there crying. I put my hands on her shoulder causing her to jump.

"It's just me." I whispered in her ear.

She relaxed immediately. I turned to look at her grandmother and now I could see why she was crying. I could tell she was once a beautiful woman, but now her left side was laxed. It looked like she had lost all feeling on her left side. Her grandmother happened to open her eyes and saw India. She tried to smile but it didn't work out to well.

"Oh baby. I'm sorry." She said but it came out like she was drunk. The womaen I remember on the phone definitely didn't sound like that. With her right hand she motioned for India to come closer. It took a minute for her to move but she did.

"Granmie." India called out laying on the bed with her.

It was then that her grandmother saw me. "Who's this fine young man with you?" She slowly got out. I guess India forgot I was there, but I wasn't mad at all. Her head popped up. She motioned for me to come over to them.

"Granmie, this is J. J stands for Jace as in the same Jace that Jalysa was dating." India said.

"Oh my damn. Girl, stop lying." Her grandmother said hitting India on her leg with her good arm. India shook her head. I chuckled a little

"I'm not lying, Granmie. And you're not going to believe this, but we found out that Jalysa use to be a man." She said hitting Granmie lightly on her arm.

Her grandmother was quiet for a minute with her eyes closed. "Granmie, did you hear me?" India asked sitting up looking at her grandmother.

"Yes baby. I heard you." Granmie said solemnly.

"Why you say it like that?" India asked with her eyebrows raised.

Her grandmother took a deep breath. She looked at me and said, "Baby you might want to take a seat. Ya'll are going to be here for a while." I looked at India who then looked at me. "Granmie, what do you have to tell me?" India asked. "Baby, get comfortable." Her grandmother said.

We walked out of her grandmother's room quietly a few hours later. We left out the hospital with so much on our mind. I wasn't prepared for what her grandmother just told us. I looked at India, and I could tell by the look on her face that she was just as surprised her damn self.

"Well what a visit that was." India said getting in the truck.

"Um yea." I replied.

"That explains a lot, I guess." She said looking at me as I climbed in.

"If you want to go back home you can. You don't have to stay out here with me. I'll let you know when I land." She said still looking at me.

"Baby, we came here together we're leaving together." I said leaving it at that. "How about we go to dinner. Something that we were already supposed to do. What do you say?" I said.

Her stomach growled. "Well, I guess you got your answer." She said laughing.

I told the driver where to go without her hearing me. While we were driving she grabbed my hand this time. I turned and looked at her. She was already smiling.

"Why are you smiling?" I asked her.

"I just wanted to say thank you. I know we started off a little different than normal, but thank you for coming with me and making it possible. I don't know how I can repay you." She said honestly.

"You can repay me by first giving me a kiss. I haven't had one since earlier. Two, you can be my girl, and move into my house that I told you about. Then, three, let me love you the way a real man should." I said looking at her with eyes that showed I wasn't lying.

She looked at me then out the window letting it down some. I laughed. "I don't know why the hell you're laughing. You just too damn smooth sometimes. I see why the women go crazy over you. But I think we can work something out." She said leaning in to kiss me.

The moment our lips touched, I thought about when we first kissed and just like that time it was something crazy. We kissed until the truck stopped in front of the Cheesecake Factory. We both looked up and the look on her face was beautiful.

"How did you know to come here?" She asked happily.

"Hell I didn't. I guessed." I said shrugging my shoulders smiling.

"Well great guess because this is my favorite spot." She said climbing out the truck before I could even reply.

****

India

Seeing my grandmother like that broke my heart so bad that I instantly started crying. I just couldn't help but think that she was going to leave me, and I was not ready for that. But like the true woman that she was, she didn't let what happened to her stop her from talking shit like usual. Even though she told us some crazy shit we had a good time. The stuff she told us had us really thinking. She really likes Jace, and I was glad about that because I like him too. It felt good to have somebody around me that Granmie actually liked. She couldn't stand Tank, so he was never allowed in or even near the house. Now thinking back on what happened, I should've just listened to my Granmie from the jump. I could've saved myself a lot of headache. But then again I wouldn't have ended up here and meetig Jace.

On the way to wherever we were going to eat, I couldn't help but be grateful that he was there with me. I didn't know what I would've done if I was by myself. I hadn't known him long, but he was already making me happy. When we got to the Cheesecake Factory, I was so happy. When I say

I love that place that's exactly what I meant. I couldn't wait to get inside. We got seated immediately. I didn't even need to look at the menu. I knew exactly what I wanted without looking. After we put our orders in, I looked up to see Jace laughing.

"What's so funny?" I asked.

"You. You wasn't joking when you said you love this place. Do you know the menu by memory?" He said.

"Actually. I do. I wasn't playing. I always eat at this restaurant. I swear I use to find any reason to come here." I said smiling.

"I can believe it." He said.

"Oh hush it. Look. I really have to thank you again for coming with me here." I said being serious.

"You don't have to thank me for anything I'm supposed to do as your man. So let's discuss this relationship of ours. First things first. You're moving into my house, right?" He said.

"I just have one question." I said looking at him suspiciously.

"And what would that be?" He asked leaning on his hands on the table.

I leaned up myself before asking my question. "What do I have to do in return? I told you I don't have any money." I said seriously.

"And I told you I got you." He replied right after.

"Why me?" I asked.

"Why not you? You're literally the first female to not fall at my feet trying to get my attention. Hell you bumped into me and wanted to take me to the hospital and not just to be close to me. You're the first female to even shoot me down. Never have I asked a female out, and they told me no. You literally told me no and walked away. If I wasn't so determined to have you, I would've kept it moving. It's just something about you that says you're the one for me. And I'm determined to figure out what it is." He said grabbing my hand.

I could tell he was serious. "Well I'll let you know when we get back with my answer. Let me just worry about my grandmother for now." I said as my phone rang. I searched in my purse for it.

"Hello." I answered seeing that it was the hospital calling. I looked at Jace with sadness before I even heard anything.

"Ms. India?" A female voice asked.

"Yes. Is everything ok?" I asked with my leg shaking. I was getting worried by the second.

"Can you come back to the hospital? Your grandmother is asking for you." The lady said.

"Of course." I said standing up immediately hanging up the phone. I was still looking at Jace.

"We have to get back to the hospital." I said.

"Ok. Go get in the truck while I pay for our stuff." He said standing up too. I nodded and walked to the truck and got in so quick. I sat there rubbing my arms with anxiety running through my body. It didn't take long for Jace to come out with our stuff. He got in and told the driver to head back to the hospital. I didn't even let the truck stop completely before hopping out and making my way to Granmie's room. I walked in and saw nurses and doctors standing around her bed.

"What's going on?" I asked walking closer to her bed. Everybody turned and looked at me sadly. The ones who were standing directly in front of her bed moved out of the way and the sight before me caused me to yell out.

"Noooooo! Please tell me she isn't gone. I can't lose my grandmother. She's all I have left. Noooo! . Please tell me this isn't so." I said looking at everybody.

A doctor walked over to me and put his hand on my shoulder. "Sweetie, calm down. She hasn't passed, but she did have another stroke while you were gone. We're all going to get out of here to give you some privacy." The doctor said. I calmed down and walked over to Granmie and grabbed her hand. She slowly turned her head towards me, looked at me, and gave me a small smile.

"Was that you who just made all that got damn noise?" She tried her best to get out in her usual voice but slurred lowly. I nodded my head.

"Yes ma'am. I thought they called me here to tell me you were gone. You know I can't handle that. You can't leave me here by myself." I told her with tears running down my face.

The door opened and Granmie and I both looked to see Jace walk in. "Come here, son." She said. He walked over and stood beside me.

"Listen here, son, because I know she isn't. I just want you to do one thing for me." She said.

"And what would that be, ma'am?" He asked.

"Take care of my baby. She's not going to want to hear this, but my time is coming. I wanted to stick around until she opened up her first shop, but I'm not. But I was here for her to meet her soulmate. I already know you're the one just don't let anything happen to her. And ya'll make sure ya'll take care of Jalysa's ass. I can feel it in my bones that that other punk ass little nigga is no longer around. There's a lot of things she doesn't know, but will find out through you. Just protect her, that's all I ask." She said. Then she turned and looked at me. I had tears rapidly running down my face. She was right I didn't want to hear that she was about to leave me.

"Baby, you know I love you with all of my heart. I want you to go home. I don't want you here when I make my transition. I am going to get cremated and my ashes will be sent to you. Know that I'm very proud of you. I want you to live out your dreams. When you get home you better find a space for your first shop. I know you don't have any money, but that's about to change. Don't ask any questions right now just listen. Like I told him, you are going to find some things out through him that he didn't even realize that he knows. Don't be afraid to love again, baby. Now ya'll gone now.

When you get the call please don't you shed another tear. You'll be given a letter, and I want you to do exactly what it says. Now give me a kiss. I love you, baby girl." She said shedding a couple tears herself. I leaned over and kissed her on her cheek. I didn't want to leave her side, but I had never disobeyed her and I wouldn't start now.

"I love you, Granmie." I whispered. I stood up and she had her eyes closed. I got out the way and Jace leaned over and gave her a kiss on her forehead.

"Thank you for giving me your baby." I heard him say.

Granmie didn't respond. I wasn't sure if she had transitioned yet or just fallen asleep. I stood there watching her until Jace pulled me out the door. The doctors and nurses stood around as we walked out. One doctor came over to me.

"She talked to us before you got here. She gave me a letter to give to you to read when you get home." He said. "For the little time she was here, she was the absolute best patient we ever had." He said walking away.

The tears hadn't stopped falling yet. I smiled the best I could said "Thank you," took Jace's hand, and walked away. We walked out the hospital getting into the truck. I was in a daze. I couldn't believe that my Granmie was going to leave me so soon. Jace told the driver to head to airport as I opened the letter.

Dear My Baby Girl,

I just want you to know that first and foremost, I love you with all of my heart. We had a connection like no other. I love you as if you were really my grandchild. Close your mouth, because I know it's open. Biologically you aren't mine. When your parents and just about everyone else in the family passed away, you were sent to me by your father's best friend. He already had a full house. He wanted to take you in just as bad as Mama Joyce did but neither of them could. I'm your father's best friend's mother, but you were raised to know me as your grandmother since both your biological grandmothers had already passed.

There was literally nobody else to take care of you. And I would've been damned if I let you become an orphan. I took you in and raised you just like you were my blood. I'm sorry that I never told you this. If you feel betrayed or lied to then I'm sorry, but I had to protect you. There were men looking for anybody connected to your father. Your father wasn't the best man out there. I hate to say this, but he got himself and your mother killed. Of course you were too young to know any of this.

I know you think that Mama Joyce is a good woman, but just know she had just as much to do with your parents' death as your father. Your father was cheating on your mother with Mama Joyce. Baby, I hate to tell you this but Jalysa was born Jayson and he or she, whatever it is, is your brother/sister. Your mother didn't know for a long time until she stumbled upon your father talking about it. He never knew she heard his conversation. Your mother went and beat Joyce's ass. That's part of the reason why she didn't take you in. Jalysa/Jayson doesn't even know this. It took your mother a long time to let you around her/him. That's why ya'll didn't meet until ya'll were teenagers. Your mother tried to keep you away from him/her for as long as she could.

Your father got into it with the wrong people, and Mama Joyce was connected to those people somehow, some way. They set your father up and then went after your mother just for the hell of it. It was a good thing you weren't home that day, because they definitely were looked for you too. I'm sure you're also probably wondering why you never had to go to a will hearing. That's because your parents knew that one day something was going to happen to them before you could even know what they really did. They also knew you would end up with me and that I would take care of you. You didn't want or need for nothing because they left everything for you with your father's best friend and he gave me all the information needed. But now that I'm about to make my transition everything that was ever your parents is now yours. And everything that was mine is yours too baby.

Baby, never give up on your dreams and love that man like he loves you. I've waited years for ya'll to finally meet. God told me he was the one for you a long time ago. Now I didn't know you were going to go through all the other shit to get to him, but I knew you were going to meet your king when you moved back there, and I'm glad you did. Always remember to keep your head up and never let anyone get in your way. Take care, baby. I'll see you on the other side. I'll say hi to your parents for you.

Love you always,
Your Granmie

I cried reading that whole letter to the point the pages were soaked from my tears. Jace's phone rang as soon as I started folding up the letter to put it back in the envelope. I wasn't paying too much attention to his conversation until he screamed "Fuck!" I looked over at him when he hung up the phone. He leaned his head back and closed his eye then ran his hand down his face.

"What's going on?" I asked.

"Man. Jalysa's ass done burned down my fucking house." He said.

Chapter 14

Jace

Granmie only confirmed what I had been thinking all this time. India was the woman for me. I was glad to have met her grandmother, but I felt bad that it was under those circumstances. I was definitely going to do what Granmie asked me to do. I mean I was going to do that anyway, but it felt good to know that I wasthe one for her. It was crazy that the older generation knew those things. I didn't know what was in that letter, but I was sure India was going to let me know sooner or later.

When I got the call about my house all I saw was red. Jalysa's ass just signed her death certificate. I hope her ass was smart enough to get ghost, because if not she was going to wish she did. We got to the hanger in no time. I helped India out the car, and we made our way to the plane. I talked to the pilots as usual and then we were off in no time. I asked the stewardess for a drink, because I needed one like yesterday. I looked over at India, who was looking at me, and then she offered a smile. I tried my best to smile back, but I couldn't because in the back of my mind I was ready to murder some damn body.

I told Jalysa she didn't want to see my other side, but she just had to bring it out of me. Before I knew it we were at the hanger back in Baltimore. I could see June and Jackson standing outside their cars leaning against them and then a third vehicle. The plane landed, I thanked the staff again, grabbed India, and we made our way off the plane. I walked towards my brothers. They both were wearing serious expressions on their faces. We did our usual handshake. They greeted India with hugs and kisses. That was when I knew that she was the one, but she needed to meet my sisters in order to get the whole approval. My brothers didn't like anybody and my sisters were just as bad, if not worse, than them.

Even though we we're all grown we tried not to let to many outsiders in our shit. That was why Jalysa never met my siblings. I knew her ass wasn't worthy of being around them, but they knew of her and had seen her on a few occasions. My sisters and June would've tore her ass into pieces so bad she would've left my ass alone. I turned to India, grabbed her hand, and walked her over to the third car.

"Look, baby,. they're going to take you back to the hotel. I need you to pack your things because you're moving today. I'm going with my brothers to handle business. I'm going to try to meet you at the house, but if not just go ahead and move your stuff in. We'll get whatever you need when I get there. Ok?" I said looking at her. She nodded her head.

"Ok." She said. I leaned in and kissed her, savoring her taste. I pulled away.

"Please be careful,." She said putting her hand on my face.

"I will." I replied helping her in the car. I hit the top of the car and it took off. I walked back over to my brothers with my game face on.

"This lovey dovey ass nigga. That was such a scene from a fucking movie. All ya'll needed was that bullshit romantic music in the background playing. Man, I can't deal with your ass and all this love. But I'm not going to lie. I'm happy your old ass finally found love." June said cracking a smile.

"Thanks nigga. I want that bitch found and found now. Let's ride out to the house." I said hopping in the car with Jackson. The moment his ass touched the seat I asked, "Bruh, what the fuck happened?"

"Man, I really can't tell you. All I know is that we gotta call that your shit was burning down. You already know we went around asking questions and shit. There's always that one person who is willing to tell it all for some money. I wasn't even tripping off coming off some bread. I wanted that info. The person said they saw the female that had been living there walk out right before the shit went up in flames. It was the simplest fucking answer ever, but it's what happened. I don't know if she left the city or not, but I put a APB out on her ass the moment I found out." He said informing me.

"That bitch know she fucked up royally. I had plans for that ass, but that's quite alright. She fucked with the right one today." I said.

I looked out the window and something caught my attention. "Bruh, is that Pops over there?" I asked.

Jackson slowed down looking in the direction I pointed to. He pulled over and we sat and watched as he talked to somebody. Our father left us when we were young. Me being the oldest, I stepped up doing what I had to do to take care of us. I wasn't going to let my family starve. My brothers and sisters didn't want for nothing. Eventually my brothers felt they were ready so they jumped in the game head first with me. We started something no one would ever be able to duplicate or take away from us. That I made sure of. The only way someone could ever take what we built away was if they killed us. Now being in the game for as long as I had, I knew bullshit when I saw it. I looked at Jackson who sat there with a mug on his face.

"I know this nigga not talking to the boys." He said.

"Looks like it." I replied. We sat and watched this nigga talk to them boys for over an hour.

"I'm going to get Janice to talk to him since they still talk and shit, and see what the hell she can find out. If this shit has to do with us, then you know the deal." I said looking back at Jackson.

"Already. You know June just needs the green light." He said.

"Oh June is going to fucking flip." I said shaking my head.

We pulled off heading towards my house. When we pulled up I swear I could've killed somebody right then and there. I looked at Jackson who looked at me and shook his head. I mean the house was still there, but you could see where the fire busted out the windows and everything. I could tell from the outside that there was nothing left on the inside. When we got out the car, I heard somebody calling my name. I looked around and saw that it was one of my neighbors, Tony. Tony was an older cat that minded his business but would say something if need be.

"What's up man?" I asked.

"Man. Where the hell have you been for the past damn day? I wish I had your number, because I have some shit to tell you." He said trying to catch his breath.

"What's going on?" I asked looking at Jackson who shrugged his shoulders. He put his hand up still trying to catch his breath.

"Damn, I'm getting old. Ok. So I know your ex was still staying here. She's not the brightest knife in the drawer, I tell you. So she's the one who set your house on fire. She wasn't even smart enough to start the shit from the inside and walk out the back door. Her ass set the shit from one of the front windows." He said pointing to which window he was talking about. "Then she tried to walk away discreetly, but then somebody yelled out to her, '"Bitch come on before somebody sees us.' " Now I know a lot of people from my day. Hell I watched ya'll grow up. But something about that voice sounded very fucking familiar. It wasn't until they pulled off that I recognized it. Jace and Jackson, I'm sorry to say this but your father had something to do with it, also. It was him in the car, and I didn't need to see his face for the confirmation. We all know that your father has a very distinctive voice, especially since his little incident some years ago." He said.

I looked over at Jackson with questionable eyes and then turned back to Tony. "What incident you talking about?" I asked curiously. "He's had that voice all of our lives. We thought that's how he always talked." I said.

"Oh no son. You ever saw the scar on his neck?" He asked. I nodded my head.

"Yea. What about it?" I asked.

"Some years back he got into a fight where the guy he was fighting cut his neck. Got part of his vocal cords. He wasn't able to talk for weeks, and when he did he ended up sounding like that. And because of what happened to him he got revenge killing the guy and his wife. I know they had a daughter, but they never found her. Yea, your pops was a little ruthless back in the day. After your mother passed is when he changed for the worse. I don't know what he's up to, but it's obviously nothing good. I just had to tell you because the shit was suspect as fuck." He said.

"I appreciate it, man." I said sticking my hand out for a handshake. He shook my hand.

"Anytime, son." He said walking off.

Jackson and I looked at each other and shook our head. "Now what did we ever do to him to make him want to hurt us in some way?" I asked aloud.

"I don't know, bruh, but we gon' find the hell out." He said. We started walking towards the house when we heard a noise behind us.

"Oh shit." We heard. We turned around to see Jalysa standing there looking like a deer caught in headlights.

"You got to be the dumbest bitch ever." I said walking over to her.

"What you doing here?" She asked shaking like rattlesnake.

"No bitch. The question is what the fuck are you doing here?" I asked grabbing her by her arm.

"I came to get some more of my stuff, but I can see that your house caught on fire." She said with a smirk.

"Yup thanks to your ass. But it's all good. You just helped me come into a lot of money. I have insurance on just about everything in that house." I said with a smile on my face wiping away the smirk from hers.

I walked her ass right over to Jackson's car. "Get the fuck in." I said putting the child lock on both doors. Jackson and I got in.

"Girl, you are really dumb." Jackson said shaking his head.

"Why the fuck would you come back to the scene of the crime your ass just committed?" He asked her turning around to look at her.

"I don't know what you're talking about. Jace told me to be out his house within a week after I get released so I did. I just came back to get some things I had left like I said." She said folding her arms and looking out the window but trying to peek out the side of her eye.

"You tried it. But it's ok you're going to pay in a minute." I said pulling out my phone to call June.

"Yea nigga?" He answered. "Meet me and Jackson at the spot. Call Tommy and Shawn." I said.

"Bet." He said hanging up. *This bitch is about to pay.*

****

Indiaa

Reading that letter really had me in my feelings. I couldn't believe Granmie wasn't biologically my grandmother. I swear I learned something new every day. I wondered if I never moved here would I have ever found out. I wondered if I would have ever found out about Tank's gay ass, or Jalysa being a fucking man at one point. Oh and the fact that shes's/he's my fuking brother/sister makes the situation even worse. I really can't believe that shit. The fact that she was able to fool Jace for all them years tops it all. Either way she was going to get what was hers. Now I had to figure out how to live my life without my Granmie. This shit was going to be harder than I thought.

When Jace put me in the car to go to the hotel, I knew he was probably up to no good. But who could blame him when his house was just set on fire. I hope he kills Jalysa's ass for this. When I got to the hotel, I went in and packed my stuff like Jace said. If I was going to let him be my man, then I guess I had to listen to him. Also I didn't want to stay in this fucking hotel anymore, especially since that bitch knew where I've been staying. I was packing for a good while when my phone started ringing. I stopped what I was doing and went looking for it.

"Hello." I answered.

"Ms. India, this is St Agnes. We wanted to call you to let you know that your grandmother has passed. We're sorry for your loss. She already told us what to do and when everything is taken care of, you'll receive her ashes." The lady said.

"Do you need my address?" I asked.

"No sweetie. You'll get informed of where to go to receive them." She said.

"Ok. Thank you for everything you guys have done. I appreciate it." I said.

"No problem. Once again we're sorry for your loss." She said.

"Thank you." I said hanging up.

I sat down and cried for what seemed like forever. Even though she told me not to shed another tear I couldn't help myself. I even laughed some thinking about how crazy she was. She always had me smiling or laughing about something.

I was sitting there laughing and crying when there was a knock at my door. Thinking it was Jace, I opened the door without looking through the peephole. I was knocked upside my head by what looked like a gun, but I couldn't tell. I tried to fight back but then somebody else appeared and put something like a cloth on my face. I fought until I couldn't fight anymore.

I woke up to darkness. I tried to touch my head but my hands were tied behind my back. I tried to stand up but my legs were tied also. I could make out that I was in some big ass room. There was only a little light, so I couldn't see anything else.

"What the hell? Where the fuck am I?" I asked aloud thinking I was by myself. Out of nowhere a light turned on and somebody sitting in a chair appeared but their back was facing me. "Who's there?" I asked squinting my eyes trying to see who it was. They got up and turned towards me. "Jace?" I asked.

"No sweetie. I'm not my punk ass son." The man said in a really deep, raspy voice.

"Ooooooookkkkkkkkk. Why am I here?" I asked.

The man walked over to me and walked around me. I followed him with my eyes until I couldn't. "Hmmmm. He picked himself a good one this time. You look familiar, though." He said squinting his eyes his damn self.

"You don't know me, sir. I can promise you that." I said.

"No, I think I do." He said. He stood there staring at me for a few minutes, but after only a few seconds I saw recognition on his face. He put his hand up to his mouth.

"Oh my shit. It's you. After all these years, I finally fucking found you. Isn't this some shit." He said walking away.

"Ummmmm excuse me, sir. What are you talking about? How do you know me?" I asked to his back. He didn't answer, he just kept walking away. He went over to the table that had the light on it and grabbed what looked like a phone.

He stood there and dialed a number. "Sir, how do you know me?" I called out again.

"Oh you're about to find out, baby. Soon. Real soon." He said with a smile on his face.

"I've been waiting years for this." He said. I guess whoever he called answered the phone.

"I fucking found her. This is going to be a two for one deal. I'll send you the address in a minute." He said and hung up. But it looked like he was dialing another number.

"Bitch, where are you? Don't try to play me. You're the one that came to me. Not the other way around. I got her ass, if you don't come the fuck on, I'm carrying this plan out without you, and you won't get shit from me." He said hanging up.

I wasn't even scared. Hell, I just lost my grandmother, the only person I had left. I just got kidnapped and it looked as if somebody wanted me dead. I wasn't about to fight shit. If it wass meant to be then so fucking be it. I sat there thinking to myself all the while he was pacing back and forth looking like he was going crazier and crazier by the minute. He kept looking at his phone. I mean every minute that passed by he was looking at his phone. I didn't know who the hell he was calling, but they damn sure wasn't picking up that phone. I was surely hoping I wasn't in this place with this crazy ass person for long, whether I was rescued or killed. I had been through enough. Too much shit has happened in these past couple of days. I was ready to just say fuck it. Next thing I knew, he was walking over to me. Before he could even reach me the door was kicked in.

"What the fuck?" The man asked.

Chapter 15

Jace

I had to call June back and tell him to grab India. I knew she would want to be there for what was about to happen. Hell, she deserved to see it. I gave him her room number. Knowing that nigga he would still beat me to the spot.

"Where the fuck are we going?" Jalysa asked.

"To meet your fucking fate. Now sit the fuck back and shut the fuck up." I yelled.

"You don't have to yell at me. I don't know what I've done to you to make you act this way towards me. All I've ever tried to do was love you and be the best girl you wanted and needed." She practically screamed back. She sat back folding her arms with a pout on her face looking out the window.

"Don't you mean man?" I asked mugging her. The look on her face said it all.

She unfolded her arms real quick and started squirming around in her seat. "I ought to beat you like the man you actually are." I said menacingly.

"Wha-wha-wha-what you talking about?" She asked trying to avoid eye contact. I was about to reply when something Jackson said caught my attention.

"The fuck you mean you got there and she's gone? The fuck? Well, keep following them and then send us all the address." Jackson said with his face screwed up.

"The fuck is going on?" I asked turning back around.

"Man, that was June. He said when he got to India's room she was gone. Her door was opened but her stuff was still there. But as he was leaving out he saw some niggas walking with a chick that looked like her, so he followed them. He's trailing them now. He's going to let us know what's up when they stop." He said. I punched the dashboard.

"FUCK!" I screamed. I ran my hands down my face.

I couldn't believe this shit. The girl finally becomes mine and already I'm fucking up by not protecting her like I said I would. Whoever did this is going to pay with so many damn bullets that they better pray real hard to God that he protects them from my guns. I just happened to look back at Jalysa since her ass got too damn quiet, and she had a damn smile on her face.

"The hell you smiling for?" I asked.

"Now you'll know what it's like to have someone taken from you. Fuck that bitch. She deserves what she gets. Shouldn't have taken my man." She said. I hauled back and punched her/him right in the fucking mouth, knocking her/him the fuck out.

"I'm sick of your mouth." I said turning back around.

"Well damn, nigga. So what you wanna do?" Jackson asked glancing at me.

I took a deep breath. "Shit we don't know where they are, so we might as well go ahead to the spot and tie this bitch up. If he calls while we're there then we'll leave her ass. She shouldn't be able to get out. Hell, I'll make sure of that." I said.

"Cool." He said and continued on the way to the spot.

The rest of the ride was quiet. We pulled up and Jalysa's ass was still knocked out. I guess I gave her a mean ass punch. Shit she deserved it. I dragged her ass inside and sat her down. I tied her ass up so good that it would take a miracle for her ass to get out. And if she does it would take a miracle for her ass to get back to civilization and survive.

The moment I got her ass tied up, Jackson's phone rang. He looked at me and said, "Let's go." I stood up and looked at Jalysa.

I punched her ass again knocking the chair over. I picked it up. She was still knocked out. I just wanted to make sure she stayed knocked out. We left out and got back in his car. He looked at his phone and put the address in his navigation system. When it popped up we looked at each other and laughed.

"You've got to be kidding me." I said.

"Wow." He said.

"There's no need to guess who it is but the question is why. I didn't even pay attention to what the address was." I said.

He turned the navigation off and then headed where we needed to go. The ride was just as quiet as the ride to the spot. When we got on the street of the address we looked for June's car. He flashed his lights at us since it was dark outside. We drove over to him and parked behind him. We all got out the car together. Tommy and Shawn was even there. They got out their cars too.

"Nigga, can you believe this nigga. Like really. I mean I was lucky to see them niggas when I did and followed them here. They aren't in there, but I know for a fact he is because he's the one who opened the door. I knew ya'll would laugh when I sent you the address." He said shaking his head.

"Funny how it's this nigga. When Jackson and I went to the house earlier Tony told us some shit you wouldn't believe." I said.

"What?" he asked looking between Jackson and I.

After I told him what Tony said this nigga started busting out laughing. "This man has been a fucking joke since before we were even here and all of our lives. I can't take him seriously." He said shaking his head.

"Look I don't have any time to waste. Jalysa's ass is tied up at the spot, and I'm hoping and praying her ass doesn't get loose. So let's get this shit over with. I can't let her be here any longer than she's already been here. She's been through enough bullshit in the past couple of hours." I said making sure my guns were fully loaded.

Everybody nodded their heads. "Shit. Everybody take an exit. Look for her. Take down whoever is in there and in the way. If any of ya'll find her before me call out for me. I wanna be the one to get her and find out what the fuck this nigga wants." I said. Everybody nodded. "Everybody strapped?" I asked looking around. Everybody nodded again. "Ight let's go." I said walking off.

I took the front door and kicked that shit in like it was nothing. I walked in with my guns out ready to shoot anything I saw moving. But I didn't see or hear shit. There wasn't a soul in sight. This nigga is dumber than I thought. Like how don't you have anybody on guard when you've kidnapped somebody.

We all ended up meeting up in the same spot. We looked at the stairs then at each other. We walked upstairs hearing this nigga's voice. I was walking closer shaking my head. He should be shot just for this bullshit alone. When we got to one of the rooms we heard his voice I kicked that fucking door in before anybody else could blink or take a breath.

****

India

When I saw Jace walk through that door happy was an understatement on how I felt. The moment his father saw him he pissed and shitted on himself.

"Oh come on. Your ass can kidnap people, but the moment you get found out unexpectedly your ass wanna get scared and shit on yourself. You're fucking nasty and stupid. I swear I wish you wasn't my father. I don't know what Ma ever saw in your weak ass." June said.

I don't know what came over their father, but he got mad and screamed. "Shut the fuck up. You don't know shit about what me and your mother had. She was and still is my world. Without her I became nothing. She made me a better man. So shut the fuck up." He screamed at them.

"Well you ain't shit now. That's what the fuck I do know. So tell me why the fuck you took my girl?" Jace asked walking over to his father with the gun raised to his head.

His father didn't move. He was frozen. And then he pissed on himself again when the gun touched his skin. "I-I-I wanted uh. I wanted uh." He stuttered.

"Oh fuck no. You was big and bad when you had her taken, but now you don't know how to fucking talk. I heard you in here being all big and bad. Now you're quiet as a fucking mouse. You've always been a weak nigga. Tony told us how you helped Jalysa burn my fucking house down." Jace said.

My mouth dropped at that moment. How could a father do that to his child? Never could I do such a thing even if my child and I weren't on good terms. The look on his father's face was just sad. Then out of nowhere I guess he got some balls.

"Fuck you, Jace. I fucking can't stand you. Never fucking could. Once she had you she worshiped the ground you, your brothers, and sisters fucking walked on. And I am going to stand here and tell you the fucking truth. I killed your mother. It wasn't fucking cancer. I poisoned the bitch. She was always so worried about ya'll that she never had time for me. So I got rid of her ass." He said. If my hands were free, I would've covered my mouth but once again it dropped.

I looked at Jace, Jackson, and June and the looks on their faces spoke volume. June ran up on his father and started beating the fuck out of him. "How fucking dare you. You took the best thing besides my brothers and sisters away from me. I can't fucking love a female, because you took her away from me. I fucking hate you." He said while he was beating him up. Jackson walked over and was about to pull him off of their father, but Jace stopped him.

"Naw let him get it out. He needs it." Jace said.

After a while we could all see that their father wasn't moving. I don't know if he was dead or just unconscious. Jace and Jackson finally decided to stop June, but he ended up stopping on his own because he got tired. He fell on his ass, pulled his knees up to his chest, laid his head on his knees, and cried. Jackson walked over to him and hugged him while Jace came over to me and untied me. As soon as I stood up I hugged him tightly. But a second later I pushed off him and looked around with my hand over my mouth.

"What's wrong, baby?" He asked. I ran to the trashcan and threw up everything I had in me then I started dry heaving. Jace came over to me and started rubbing my back.

"Are you ok?" He asked.

I shook my head. Because I had been through this before, I knew what was up. I put my head down. He leaned down and lifted my chin.

"Are you ok?" He asked. I looked around. Nobody was really paying us any attention.

"I'm pregnant." I whispered. He let my chin go.

"What you say?" He asked backing up some. I looked him in his eyes.

"I'm pregnant." I said a little louder. He just looked at me for a couple minutes.

"How do you know?" He asked.

"I was pregnant before remember? I remember when my ex and I did it. We were using condoms up until I got pregnant. The time he didn't use one, I threw up the next damn day and didn't stop. I don't get sick. I know my body." I said with my eyes watering up. I was hoping he wasn't going to deny my baby.

"Ok. Well, we need to go to the doctor ASAP then." He said smiling.

Involuntarily the tears started to run down my face anyway. "Why are you crying?" He asked.

"Because I just knew you were going to think I was crazy. It's not normal for females to know they are pregnant this fast. I guess I'm a rare case, but I didn't think you would believe me." I said.

"I told you I got you, baby. You don't ever have to wonder with me. I'm gon' always have your back." He said kissing me. I was smiling on the inside.

"Ok you fucking love birds. I'm happy I'm finally about to get my fucking niece or nephew, but can we get rid of this nigga please. We still got a bitch at the spot who's probably trying to escape right now." June said standing up. The two guys that were with them picked up their father and walked out before us. A few minutes later we finally left out the house.

As soon as we walked out we were swarmed by hundreds of police officers. "Jace, Jackson, and June Vincent you are under arrest for the murder and disappearance of Trey Hamilton." A beautiful lady said walking up to us in a FBI jacket. Then two other officers came walking up, and they all began handcuffing Jace and his brothers.

"Charmaine, this some bullshit and you know it." June said being jerked around by the lady.

"You have the right to remain silent. Anything you say or do can and will be used against you in the court of law. You have the right to an attorney. If you cannot afford one, then one will be appointed to you. Do you understand?" She asked June.

"Charmaine, if you don't get these fuck ass cuffs off me then you gon' know something. Now I don't know what kind of shit you on, but you need to hop off. I don't know why the fuck you have a such a hard on for me over a fucking fling. Damn, you knew how I got down. Don't be mad at me cuz you caught feelings for a nigga." He said loudly.

I guess she got mad because she threw his ass against the car and began frisking him roughly. I was so confused. "Baby, stay by the phone." Jace said getting my attention.

"Tommy. Shawn, take care of this and look out for Janicka and Janice. Ya'll make sure she always good,." he said nodding his head towards me to as they walked over to us. I don't know what they did with the guys father and how they were able to get cose to us. I stood there with my arms wrapped around my body. I couldn't believe this shit.

Chapter 16

Jace

I couldn't believe this shit. If it wasn't one thing it was another. I was sitting at this fucking table, five months later, waiting for India to visit me. India had another fucking doctor's appointment that I missed. She was supposed to find out what we we're having. I couldn't believe that I was in here and my girl was out there by her fucking self. I knew her grandmother was looking down at me fucking pissed. I was missing the growth of my baby. Well not really but then again I was.

India came to see me faithfully every weekend. She wore a smile on her face every time, but her eyes showed sadness. I must admit I had a strong ass woman. What my brothers and sisters didn't know was that the moment I got transferred to the prison, I married her as. I knew it wasn't how she wanted to get married but I had to. She was mine the moment I met her. Her grandmother just confirmed the feeling I had.

The first day she came to see me she brought me the letter she was given when we were at the hospital. After reading it I couldn't stop apologizing. She stopped me at one point and said I had no reason to be sorry. It wasn't like I was the one who did it or knew. I couldn't believe how we had been connected all this time. The good thing that came out of some of this was that India was given a check from her grandmother with more than enough money to live off of. She was able to finally open up her first shop. She had been living her dream of doing hair from the moment she got the check. She found the perfect spot downtown and, with the help of my sisters, has the biggest clientele in the state. I couldn't be more proud of my baby.

Things didn't get any better for my family within this time frame. Jackson's ass didn't do much time since they didn't have anything on his ass really. And I wasn't even mad. One of us needed to be out there running shit. And like the boss he was, the Three Kings Cartel was running better than ever. Hell even our clubs were doing well, still. Jackson was a business man at heart. I think he was considering retiring. Hell I was too. I had a family to think about now. But Jackson's ass has a story of his own. Just wait on it. And if you're wondering what happened to my father then let Jackson's ass tell you, because he can tell you what really happened..

June's ass cussed Charmaine out from the moment she arrested his ass until he was sentenced. Shit wasn't pretty for his ass, but what do you expect from a bad boy like him. But I'll let him tell his story later. Oh ya'll better believe that we're still going to have our summer bash. And I'll leave it at that. Oh and Jalysa's ass? Shit I don't even know. That shit is a fucking mystery right now.

My baby came walking up to me looking just as beautiful as ever. "Hey, Mr. Vincent." She said leaning down to give me a kiss.

"Hi there, Mrs. Vincent. How was the appointment?" I asked.

"Well, I mean it went well, but somebody didn't want to open their legs, but I have even bigger news." She said beaming. I sat there looking at the love of my life and wondered what I did to deserve such a kind hearted, smart, beautiful woman.

"Baby. You hear me?" She said getting my attention.

"I'm sorry, baby. I was just looking at the most beautiful woman in the world wondering why she's sticking by my side?" I said.

She sat up, then stood up, and walked around to my side. She sat down on my lap. "Not because you saved me. Not because you didn't hassle me. Not because of what happened to me. But because you loved me through my flaws. You've done for me just as much as my Granmie had did for me. You don't take anything but my love from me, and don't ask for anything in return. I'm blessed to have a man so genuine and loving. Not to mention handsome. I love you with everything in me. WE love you. All three of us." She said then got up and sat back down in her seat.

She sat there looking at me. Then it hit me what she said. "What you mean the three of us?" I asked.

"Twins." She said cheesing hard.

"You're lying." I said gleaming. She shook her head.

"One was hiding the whole time, but then decided to pop up on the screen today. Not only that, their heartbeats were beating at the same time all this time. Today we could hear them both. Can you believe it?" She said. I stood and walked over to her side, picked her up, and spun her around.

"I'm having twins." I yelled out. I couldn't believe it.

After spinning around for a few minutes, I finally stopped and put her down. I swear nothing could take the joy away that I was feeling. We sat back down smiling hard. "So how's the salon?" I asked.

"Oh, baby, everything is going great. Business couldn't be better. But I keep getting letters on my car and I don't know who and where they're coming from. I brought them with me to show you." She said digging in her bag. She pulled them out and handed them to me. It was a good couple of them, too.

"When the hell did you start getting these? and why the fuck am I just now seeing and hearing about this?" I asked getting mad. She sat back and began rubbing her stomach, something she did when she was getting upset.

"I went to Jackson about it, and he's looking into it, but I knew I should tell you, too. It's only been a few days, but if you look at them then you would see that they are dated from a long time ago. I don't know what to think of it." She said still rubbing her stomach.

Before I could answer a body appeared to the side of our table. "Well, well, well. Now look what we have here. Now isn't this a beautiful sight." The person said.

"I thought you were dead." I said. I looked at India who was looking at this person with her mouth open.

"I guess it wasn't in God's plans for me to die." They said.

"What the fuck are you doing here, Jalysa?" India asked.

"I'm glad you asked." She said taking it upon herself to take a seat. She went in her bag and pulled out an envelope.

"Let's talk." She said.

"I don't have shit to say to you." I said.

"Oh but you do." She said opening the envelope and pulling out what was inside. She laid some pictures out on the table. I looked around making sure nobody was close enough to see what was going on.

"Oh my God. Are you fucking kidding me?" I heard India say. I quickly looked down at the pictures she pulled out. The shit I was looking at was fucking crazy. I couldn't believe what I was looking at.

"How?" I asked.

Jalysa stood up and the next thing you know she had a gun pointing at me. "Ahhhhhh." India screamed.

"What the fuck?" I said. *This bitch is bold.*

"Put the gun down, ma'am." One of the guards said.

"You hurt me. You shamed me. I now have nobody. You deserve everything that happens to you." She started.

"I'm not going to tell you again. Put the gun down."
Another guard said. The next thing you know India stood up.

POW! POW! POW!

"Nooooooo!."

To Be Continued…………………..

CPSIA information can be obtained
at www.ICGtesting.com
Printed in the USA
LVHW011930160719
624288LV00008B/127/P